The Dog Under The Bed 2

Arthur On the Streets

DJ Cowdall

http://www.davidcowdall.com
https://twitter.com/djcowdall
https://www.facebook.com/DJCowdall

Other Works By DJ Cowdall

Novels

Missing

The Dog Under The Bed

Two Dogs In Africa

Hypnofear

I Was A Teenage Necromancer: Book 1

I Was A Teenage Necromancer: Book 2: Supernature

The Magic Christmas Tree

The Kids of Pirate Island

53%

Short Stories

Inferno
Kites
Sacrifice
A Breath of Magic

Available from all good booksellers

Acknowledgements

Edited by Adam Luopa.
https://luopa.com/

Cover Art by Olivia
Pro Design

CHAPTER ONE

Well, dear reader, here we are again, about to hear more stories of our favorite friend, Arthur. Now however, we shall have to travel back in time a little, well, not literally, but back in the memories of times gone by, back when Arthur was young, and back before he found a cozy little home under a little boy's bed.

Now obviously, we all know Arthur's story, of how he came to be running around like a terrified rabbit, running this way and that, and how we ended up. This story tells us of his trials and tribulations, of how he survived and what he learned, good and bad, on the streets.

Now we know Arthur is at times a clever and crafty little dog, and we know all too well how foolish he can be, but little is known of just how much of a survivor he is, and all that he has had to overcome in life, simply to stay alive. Let us share his journey together, and no doubt share a tear here and there for all that he has seen and done.

So one fine day at the back end of summer, there was Arthur, living a fragile if contented life, with someone he has loved all his life, in peace, comfort and happiness. Then what happens? It all changes so quickly, he can barely keep up. Being such a sensitive little dog, and so instinctive, he is fully aware that time is moving on, not just for him, but for those whose lives he feels so deeply connected to, he cannot imagine anything else. Then comes that one moment, that one singular moment which changes everything, as it does for so many of us, and then nothing is ever the same again. For a loving little dog, such sudden, abrupt differences can be bewildering. Nobody talks to dogs when the only people they have ever truly loved are suddenly gone, nobody tells them what the plans are, everyone is too busy trying to sort out their own things, and sadly for dogs like Arthur, not only do they come last, they are often forgotten.

Now we know Arthur is a lucky dog, because he has survived, and like so often in life, doing so takes a little bit of luck, but it also takes plenty of courage, not to mention hard work. Arthur has been lucky to find others as loving as he is, but not before a never-ending search, each and every day.

Let me begin, only this time, not at the beginning, well OK, yes it is at the beginning, but also in a way in the middle, because we're going to talk about everything he went through, good and bad, happy and sad, the ups and downs, many, many downs of life for any dog, on the streets, alone.

CHAPTER TWO

Arthur liked to run, along with eating and sleeping, it was always the best part of his day. Of course, a nice cuddle with Mother was always wonderful, but the feel of running in the fields was something different to anything else in his life, where he came alive and felt as young as a puppy again.

This one particular day, things had been quiet in the house, but the old lady who loved him so much had barely spoken, not even dressed that day, and unusually never even filled his bowl with water. She had simply gone to sit down in her favorite chair, where he wandered over to be at her feet, or more likely on her feet, because he loved sitting on people's feet.

The end of summer had brought with it a change in the air, which reflected in the house. The temperature had dropped outside, but inside there was more than just a chill, even the emotion felt different.

As always, Arthur was sat on the old lady's feet, but for some reason he couldn't stop shaking, or shivering, his whole body trembling with it, which was new to him, because he had never experienced it before. Deep down he knew something was wrong, but being so carefully protected and sheltered, so well provided for by such a loving woman, he was the picture of confusion.

A darkness came upon the room, the air falling still, and Arthur's coat tingled all over. In the moment he grew a little older himself, a little more mature, but also afraid. He stood up, looking at the old lady, looking for that little twinkle in her eye, the one that shared her smile with as much joy for love and life as anything else he could imagine. Now she just kept her eyes closed. Arthur waited, and waited, nudging her hand fallen to her side. She felt like the air in the room, not quite so warm as he was used to.

All of his senses were alive, the trembling grown worse than ever. Arthur let out a little yelp, but heard nothing except the ringing of his own cries. He trotted to the end of the living room, looking out into the hall, wondering who he could call. There was nobody. He trotted back, sat once again at her feet, and waited. His mind was rolling over, thinking of all the fun, thinking of food, thinking of running. Then he thought of her, such a sweet, beautiful woman, and how much he wanted one of those fine hugs again.

The door, someone opened it, and he leapt up. A man walked in, the look on his face, something Arthur had never seen before. Arthur shared the emotion, but something different, such a sense of panic. The man dropped to his knees beside the old lady, taking her hand. Then he made such a terrible noise, so stricken, that Arthur truly panicked, unsure of what to do. He stepped away, trotted across the room, looking at them, his mind a mess of ideas and emotions.

Nobody talked to Arthur, nobody told him what was going on. He could deep down, instinctively, feel the sadness washing over them.

It was fine, there was always a reason to be happy. He could eat, but there was no food, perhaps a hug, but no one looked at him, perhaps a sleep, but he was trembling too much to allow it.

Of course, his last favorite treat, going for a big run. He would do that, and take it all in, and when it was over, she would do what she always did, clap her hands and tell him how much she loved him.

Arthur ran down the hall, out into the bright sunshine, and down the street. The more he ran, the more he panted, the more his heart beat, and he could feel better. It was fun to run, the best thing in the world.

He would run, and run, and carry on, until the old lady clapped her hands and called for him, to share her love.

The old lady never clapped her hands again, and Arthur never stopped running.

CHAPTER THREE

What a day. So much fun. Was there anything to compare to going outside for any dog? Someone throws the ball, then he runs and gets it, brings it back, and then refuses to hand it over. That was always how he loved to do it, because it was as much fun to toy with his best mate as it was to run and get the ball. Unfortunately, now there wasn't a ball, but no matter, because what mattered was he knew the way, down the road, left through the small road at the side, to a small passage lined by trees all the way. Then under the underpass, beneath the busy road which he must never go on, and down a small, back country lane. Then, time for the adventure.

The field at the bottom opened out into a large area of lush wild grass, and equally wild flowers. The colors at that time of year were always stunning, vibrant reds, deep flecks of purple, and a haze of never ending yellow, as tall stalks of flowers swayed this way and that, undulating in rhythm with the light breeze.

Arthur's ears flapped a little as he ran, his mouth open just enough that he could pant and breathe, releasing a torrent of hot air with each happy bound. The grass was soft underneath his paws, like a natural carpet pushing against him, providing a light, uplifting spring with each touch. Even the air smelled sweet, like sugary food cooking on the stove, wafting into his long black whiskered nose, reminding him that he could be happy after all.

Eventually the stream came into view, a long, winding little passage of water that glittered in the sun. Beneath its clear surface was a path of pebbles, leading so far into the distance that Arthur had to squint in the heavy sun. The other way led to a forest, burgeoning trees, listing easily in the high winds up above.

He slowed a little, feeling the need to do something about the heat, and the nagging thirst in his mouth. All the while in the back of his mind was the need not to go too far, don't go near the road, but still, he was thirsty. Slowly he dropped down the small grassy bank, covered on both sides by dark, swaying greenery. It cooled as he moved closer, until he met the edge of the slowly flowing water, its cold iciness wrapping itself around his muddy brown paws. He stepped in, feeling the gravel give way, sliding just a little deeper, as he leaned over, head down, allowing the tip of his muzzle to touch the water. Arthur opened his mouth, rudely stuck out his tongue, and lapped away, as if he were trying to drain the world's biggest bowl of water.

Minutes passed as he drank deeply, filling his belly so much it began to feel like a soft barrel, sloshing around with every move he made.

Something caught his attention, out of the corner of his eye, a blurred yellow flash. He could never resist anything moving quickly, it didn't matter what it was, as long as it sped away, because then he knew it must want to play, to run and play. *Run, Arthur, run*, it called to him. So off he went.

Arthur splashed loudly in the water as he attempted to cross to the other side, to find what was running from him. White rafts of stream water splashed all over, soaking his fur at his back, reminding him how cold it was in contrast to such a lovely day. It didn't matter, because he was warm from so much running, and his mind was different to how it had been earlier, so much happier, that all he could think about was continuing like it, forever if possible.

He ran up the bank, stopped to shake the excess water off, looking like a jumper in a spin dryer, sending plumes of water all over, kindly watering the plants as he did so. Then he saw it, the rabbit, stopped for a moment to catch his eye. He could tell it wanted to have fun. Usually the old lady would refuse to allow him to run so far, but she was quiet for the moment, she didn't seem to mind, so off he went, looking back at the little bundle of fur, sitting there, waiting to be chased some more.

Arthur barked, something he rarely ever did. He was mostly such a shy little dog, wary of strangers, and never wanting to upset anyone by being so loud and boisterous, but today was special, he had found a new friend, and so bark he would. Yap, yap, yap he went.

The rabbit was fast, at times too fast. Nothing could run faster than Arthur, but this little bunny had a clever way of dodging and weaving, in and out of trees, up small hills and through bushes. Arthur tried to copy it, sprinting along, headlong into a bush, cracking his head on the main stem and bouncing off, rolling away. It was fine, he had a thick head, he could bounce all he liked and wouldn't mind.

On he ran, until the rabbit stopped at a small open space, beside a series of wooden sticks with metal wire running attached to them. It waited until he caught up with it, watching. It was a perfect welcome for him to nip at it, and roll around in the grass, pawing each other, but the rabbit had other ideas, in a flash disappearing down a dark hole in the ground.

Arthur just stood, looking in, peering into the darkness, waiting for it to pop its head back out. He waited, and then waited some more, until an idea trickled into his head. This new friend of his was gone, and probably not coming back.

With perfect timing, his tummy began to rumble, sending out a long, feeble gurgling, telling him it was time for tea. Arthur looked up, trying to see if the old lady had followed him, but unusually she hadn't. He had been foolish, spoiled by too much fun, not looking where he was going. Taking in a deep breath, he sat down, looking up, his nose tilting rapidly up and down as he breathed in gulps of fresh, warm air.

As he looked around, he couldn't help but notice how dark it had grown. Across the fields and trees around, it looked clear and sunny, but shadows had begun to grow, and the trees sheltering him now seemed to darken everything around him. He never enjoyed being out late, always wanting to do his business out in the back garden before quickly getting back into the comfort and warmth. He would have to get going, back to the lady, back home.

Wearily, he stood up. All that hard work running, that chasing, and the type of day it had been, he simply wasn't used to it. All Arthur could think about was the soft, fluffy round bed, the one with the old lady's slipper in it, and some half-chewed toys, the one where like nowhere else on Earth, he felt safe, a home.

With no time to waste, off he went, tracking ahead, before stopping to look back. The silence was unusual, no road traffic, no talking, not even the sound of animals. The same sense of uncertainty began to drift into him, making him wonder what to do. As he looked ahead, he saw everything darkening, and yet so green, but when he looked the other way, it all seemed darkening too, and equally green. The wire and wood fence ran along in both directions, and bushes and trees opposite from there. He had two choices which way to go, but he couldn't remember either of them. All of his attention was on the rabbit. For the first time in his life, Arthur was genuinely frightened.

"Hey," someone shouted. Arthur's ear suddenly pricked up and his heart leapt, filling him with joy. She had come for him, coming to bring him that amazing hug, that wonderful sense of safety and belonging.

He stood, his head flicking this way and that, trying to hear for it again, to see where it had come from.

"Hey," the voice called again. Now he knew, it was from the other side of the fence, calling for him. Without another thought he ran to the fence, pushed his head under the lowest piece of wire, then dragged himself down until his body hugged the cooling grass. Closest to the fence, the grass was thick and wiry, but he was strong, and pushed with all his might. Finally, the damp-ridden wood cracked, pushing the wire fence up, allowing him to move freely.

"Come on, this way," a voice shouted, even louder now.

Arthur could barely contain his excitement, as he sprang away from the fence. Without seeing it he came right to the top of a large rolling drop, a huge hill stumbling all the way down to the edge of a forest. He stopped to hesitate, finally thinking about things, but before he could do the sensible thing, his front paws gave way, sending him in a twirl of spinning light and dark.

Over and over he rolled, falling down the hill, feeling every single bump and twig underneath as he rolled. Arthur stuck out a paw, tried to twist quickly, sought to grab at the ground, but it was no good, it was too steep, he was moving too quickly.

He thought any moment a huge crash would come, as he hit something hard, but instead he just rolled onto flat ground, right up to the base of a tree.

Arthur did his favorite trick- feeling slightly embarrassed, he jumped up, shook quickly, and looked around, seeing if anyone had been watching him. He snorted out a great breath of annoyance, before allowing himself to be relieved that he was alone. Pride was fully intact.

No matter, it was all a bit of fun, but now time for home. For a moment he listened, waiting for the voice, but it never came. All he could feel was a new chill in the air and an increasing darkness all around. One side of him lay the steep bank he had rolled down, the other a dense blanket of trees. The bank was too steep to climb back up, leaving only the trees ahead and around. Neither option seemed particularly good.

Arthur stood for a moment, wondering what to do. His stomach rumbled even louder, reminding him it was way past food time. Needs must, he began to walk slowly towards the trees. A fine scent of pine lifted the air around him, reminding him of late summer, but also of how much he loved being outside. How much he loved it would soon be put to the test.

The forest was dense, with low hung trees, branches stuck out in all directions, making passage difficult. Arthur didn't want to be here, or have to carry on, and for the first time in as long as he could remember, he felt properly alone.

Regardless, he was still a brave dog, and would carry on, one thing on his mind: to get home and soon. He began walking quicker, ignoring each branch as it tugged on his fur, catching his legs, swiping his tail, catching his collar. He pushed on, deeper and deeper, until it became so dark he could hardly see. A sudden, unusual sound caught his attention, forcing him to stop, as branches to and fro held onto him like a wooden safety net. His ears pricked as it came again, a chirping noise followed by a cooing sound. It was nothing, thankfully.

On he continued, wondering if he had made a mistake. He stopped, looking back, quickly turning his head as his whiskers twanged on flecks of branch end, signaling him that he would be stuck any moment, and then there would be no turning back.

Then it came, the glimpse of hope, a small slither of light just off to his left. It was slim, not very bright, but for now was all he had. Arthur closed his eyes and pushed with all his might, feeling the pine needles underfoot dragging at him, his nostrils full of the fragrant air, but nothing would stop him.

He burst out into the dying embers of the sunlight drifting across the horizon, as the forest ended. He was at the one place he knew he should never go to, a road, dangerous and noisy.

Once again it was a simple choice. He could either go back to the forest, or on to the road, which wasn't much of a choice. One would be getting stuck, the other getting told off for being so naughty. Arthur stood, and whimpered. He didn't like letting the lady down, but what could he do?

Slowly he walked down the slight grass recess, out onto the road. It was warm to the touch from the hours of hot sun. At least it didn't prickle him like the pines had. The road went off in either direction, but he couldn't decide which way.

There it was, finally, something he recognized. A short way ahead, down the road, a bright yellow bush, and beside it a colorful picture. Arthur had no idea what the picture was, but he knew it, he had seen it when walking with the lady, it was the way home.

Arthur broke out into a run, heading down the road, forgetting that he wasn't to go on there. As he approached, he noticed the sign and the yellow bush lay at the front of a piece of grass, spreading out left and right. He would go left, heading down the small road. It made sense, because it was how she always took him, that side of the path, allowing others to pass. That was why he was such a good dog, so well mannered, because of her.

Arthur gently wandered around the curving road, looking intently, seeking out anything else. Again, he spotted it, something else he recognized, such luck, a bin, a green one, taller than he was, one that he so much enjoyed lifting his leg on. Arthur chased towards it, continuing to look for things he knew. Everything was turning out so much better, he was seeing things he knew well, on his way home. Any moment the lady would call out for him, and before he knew it, he would be home, full tummy, all back to normal.

To his right, once again he spotted yet another reminder, a bench, something the lady often sat on. The moment he saw it he lit up, so happy at the thoughts that she might be there, or near. Then, there it was again, another reminder, run fast, because the more he saw the closer he was to home. He ran, right up to the yellow bush and the sign, then on, to the bin, then to the bench, then to the bush, and on and on, until a huge noise screamed at him, beeping again and again followed by a screeching sound.

Arthur no longer followed the reminders, instead fleeing off to the side of the road, ignoring the car, parked, as the people inside looked at him.

Finally, feeling exhausted, Arthur just walked, following the side of the road, until he saw a passage with a pathway, leading up to some houses. Nothing seemed as he remembered, but he was still hopeful.

Night was falling, darkness enveloping him, but it wasn't all bad, because filling his nose was the most wonderful smell, the kind he had often shared with the lady, fish and chips. It called to him, and off he went in search.

CHAPTER FOUR

"That will be ten pounds and fifty five pence, please."

"Hey, have the prices gone up?"

"No, these are the cheapest prices around, I dare you to find cheaper."

Steven handed over two crinkled notes, before dropping coins onto the counter, counting each penny as he went, as if it were the last money in the world to him. Being only twelve years old, and about to spend so much of his Gran's money, he almost trembled in anticipation at what was to come.

Just as he was about to grab his bags of freshly cooked food, the chippie stopped him. "Hold your horses, it's short," he insisted, hand on the top of the wrappers.

"No, it's all there, I counted it."

The chippie lifted his hands, dropping the pound note and coins back onto the glass counter. One by one he counted off, first the note, then the silver coins, then the copper coins.

"Ten pounds, fiftyyyyyyy, fifty one, fifty two, fifty three. See, I told you it was short."

Steven looked up at the man serving him, or refusing to, then down at the chips. "That's all I have, I only had exact money," he pleaded.

"No cash, no chips, sorry," the chippie insisted.

Feeling dejected, Steven began to look around, feeling in his jacket pockets, hands in his trousers, desperate. He could feel the hunger in his stomach, almost drooling at the prospect of a full mouth and a full tum.

Just as he was about to beg to be let off for the two pence he was short, something nudged his leg. He looked down to see a spritely, happy looking brown dog looking back up at him. He was panting, but wide eyed, as if to say *hurry up and pay and let's get eating.*

Steven felt shocked, not only to see the dog next to him, but that anyone would let a dog into a chip shop.

"Hey, you can't bring dogs in here," the chippie insisted. Steven looked up at him, confused, then back at the dog.

Arthur stepped back a little, but refused to take his gaze off either of them. He was hungry, it was tea time, hurry up and serve it, he thought.

As the dog stepped back, a round copper coin came into view on the floor. "There it is, the two pence, I must have lost it," Steven called, smiling finally.

As he leaned over to pick it up, Arthur's tail began to wag furiously, as he welcomed the kind offer of food.

"Hey, I told you, no dogs, and don't come in here and stroke it, now leave," the chippie shouted, grabbing at the bags of food and walking away.

"But... but, he's not," Steven began to plead.

"I said out, and take that mangy mutt with you."

Arthur simply stood looking up at the shocked and confused boy, wondering how long he would have to wait to be fed.

Steven tried to offer one last attempt at allowing his chips to be taken. "But..."

"Stop calling me butt, goodbye," the chippie said one last time, taking the packs of chips and dropping them behind the counter. For good measure, he plucked out one chip from the sitting basket, as if to rub it in, but as he dropped it into his mouth, he instantly realized it was too hot and dropped it on the floor.

There was nothing else for it. Steven took his money from the counter and walked out, glancing back to the owner then to Arthur.

Arthur followed, his tail still wagging as if he was excited by what was to come.

"I don't know what you're waiting for, neither of us is getting fed," Steven insisted. Arthur had no idea what he meant but was getting impatient for food.

Outside the shop it was completely dark, except for rows of street lighting, amber colors reflecting against the shop window. The air still offered a cool breeze, but a fragrant air brought with it a suggestion that things might change.

As Steven walked away, wondering what to do, whether to go to the local Morrison's superstore and buy in tea, Arthur trotted along behind him. All the while he kept his bright eyes on the young man, ever hopeful of a wonderful turnout.

"Sorry, doggie, but you can't go with me," Steven said, trying not to be too abrupt. He could see the dog had been looked after well, his coat well groomed, and he had obviously been well fed, his little tummy hanging down from so much food and so little proper exercise.

Arthur had never been shown the meaning of *no*, it was an alien concept to him, where being denied something was usually a game just before the treat came out.

As the two walked on further, up past Priestley College, Arthur continued to bound along, occasionally looking out to see if it were somewhere he recognized. So far, he knew nothing of it. One of the things he had experienced from being with the only woman he had ever known and loved was that she had her habits, places she went, where she took him, so limited even if they were all the fun in the world to him.

As they walked, Arthur took in all the sights, all the new and unusual things he had never been of mind to think of. The pair came up to some tall black things full of shiny lights, each changing frequently, from red to orange and then green. To Arthur they were pretty, but nothing as bright as the colors or different others would see, but they were still amazing to him, so different to anything he was used to. To him these were symbols of Warrington's unique majesty and color. Why they changed didn't matter, all that stood out was they were pretty, and depending on how they looked, others would stop and watch them too.

As one light went to green, a small picture of a man that looked like Steven appeared, and once again they were off, walking in procession as the young boy headed up the hill alongside the road. Arthur followed in line, as if they were marching on to some great adventure. It was almost too much fun, but still in the back of his mind he had to get home. He would, soon.

The bright yellow signs of the superstore came into view, as neon lit up all around. Arthur's eyes sparkled in the glow of it, as cars passed to and fro quickly.

Steven was fully aware that he was being followed, but hoped if he carried on and ignored the new friend, he might get bored and walk away. The last thing he wanted was for its real owner to suddenly spot him walking away with their prized pet and come running after him shouting.

The front of the store was all a glow and brightly lit. It was a spectacle to Arthur, something he had never quite experienced before. Twice he had been lucky enough to ride in a car with his owner, but he had never been allowed into such an amazing place.

"Stop now, go on, you can't come in here with me," Steven insisted, waving his arm at him, trying to shoo him away.

To Arthur it was much, much more, it was an invitation to join the fun, roll up, come on in, run around, sample the delights. So he did. Before Steven could get through the wide-open doors Arthur shot through, scarpering in past the circus of shoppers, into the main area. Ahead were rows and rows of fresh, shiny looking vegetables, but the air was much cooler. Occasionally shoppers would stop, some with trolleys, some with baskets, looking at the manic little brown dog, as it scurried this way and that.

It was like all his birthdays had come at once. Who needed chips when all of this food was available? Arthur stopped at a wooden table, jumping up to sniff at a pack of freshly baked white rolls. If they tasted as good as they smelled, he was in for a treat.

Steven walked past, looking at the dog from the corner of his eyes, hoping he wouldn't be seen, hoping against hope that no one would ever think that dog was his.

"Hey, you can't bring a dog in here," a voice shouted. It sounded deep, mean, and determined. Steven looked around to see a man in a white coat, and for a moment thought he was being chased by a doctor.

As he came to his senses the man in the white coat charged past him, making it obvious he was a store manager.

"Fancy bringing a dog into a shop," a woman said. Steven turned to look at her, to see an elderly lady, dressed in a light blue coat several sizes too large, wearing high heels to shop in, clinging onto her basket of three items as if it might prove a shield against the wild dog.

"It's not mine," Steven pleaded meekly, but as he was learning, nobody seemed to listen to such things. Words never had any meaning when people could see what they wanted to see.

Arthur was in his element, as he ran from one table to the next, then further along to a side counter, containing chilled pizzas. Should he grab one, get stuck in, he wondered, or should he move on? There, across on the other side, counters of such smelly fish, and further along, meat, pies, all sorts. It was too much, overload to his senses. Home was forgotten as his mind washed up in a frenzy of fabulous food!

"Stop," a voice called loudly, but Arthur was too excited to stop anything.

"Will you please get your dog and take him out of here," a man demanded. Steven turned to see a short man dressed in a baggy black suit with Security written on it in silver letters. The man appeared far too large to run, so didn't even bother trying, instead turning his focus on an easier target.

"No, you see," Steven began to say.

"Sir, please do not say no, do not refuse to remove your animal from the store, it is a health and hygiene issue," the security man continued, struggling to give life to words in between struggling for puffs of breath.

The manager that looked like a doctor ran after Arthur, leaning over, hand out, ready to grab at his bright red collar. To Arthur it was a sign that he wanted to play, so ran even faster. As he slipped across the shiny floor, his paws struggled for grip, his claws clicking quickly on the ground, refusing to help him move along. Just as the manager was about to grab him once more, Arthur slid, headlong, his paws acting as mere supports, as he crashed heavily into a huge pile of neatly stacked tins. None moved, not one, as Arthur looked up at them, hundreds of pictures of the same cow on the side, all best beef. Apart from the cow, which he knew of well due to his days running in the fields, he had no idea what was in it. Crisis averted, Arthur leapt up and once again began his pursuit of splendid food from all over. As he walked quickly away, the manager slid in beside him, also skidding into the tins. He held on, hands in the air, teetering, desperately struggling not to knock the entire collection everywhere. Miraculously, nothing fell, and the man stopped just in time.

A little boy stood watching from the safety of his mother's trolley, wide eyed at the show on offer. It was amazing, a little doggy and a man in a white coat chasing all over.

"Charlie, stay out of the way," the boy's mother insisted, as her attention remained fixed on the price of a packet of butter in the near fridge. It was on offer, but even better with a coupon. It was a good day for her, saving money was always good with a five year old boy to raise.

Charlie ignored his mother's wise advice, too much having fun watching the dog and the man play together. As the man slid and stopped, and turned to go after the dog again, Charlie walked away from the protection of the trolley, up to the huge stack of tins, holding out his hand to look at the picture of the pretty cow.

"Charlie, come back over here," his mother insisted, still holding onto the pack of butter.

"No, go do as you're told," the man in the white coat pleaded.

"Hey you, don't you tell my son what to do," the woman shouted.

Charlie ignored him, picking out a can from the bottom of the stack, much to the manager's horror. Everyone watched as the cans shook. Charlie stood up, wandering back to Mummy.

"Oh, thank goodness," the manager insisted, breathing out a sigh of relief, wondering once more where the dog had gone.

Charlie's mother glared at him. "I don't like anyone telling my son what to do except me," she insisted, picking Charlie up and placing him into the trolley seat. As she continued to glare at the man, she swung her trolley around, deliberately missing the manager. She was in a mood, and walked away feeling angry.

The man in the white coat stood, struggling for what to say as Charlie's mother swung the trolley back, hitting the corner of the stack sending hundreds of tins scattering all over. She never looked back, muttering to her son about the cheek of some people.

Completely ignoring the fuss, Steven went on about his business as he had intended. The fuss was someone else's problem now, he would just do what had to be done and get gone. He quickly grabbed a small basket, added a few food items he needed before heading for the checkout. The last thing he noticed was a little brown dog running around the aisles being chased by one man in a white coat and three others in green uniforms. All he could think was he was glad he wasn't one doing the chasing after that crazy dog.

All done, Steven picked up his plastic bag of food and quickly went outside. He felt relieved, finally alone again, as he could once again get back to walking to his Gran's, and cooking them a lovely meal, just for the two of them. It wasn't always easy, being expected to do so much for his elderly Grandmother, given his young age, but on nights such as that they both enjoyed it, and he genuinely looked forward to them.

A late wind had picked up, bringing with it a cooling breeze. He felt the suspicion of impending rain, and hurried along all the quicker for it. The last thing he wanted was to get wet.

A few hundred yards ahead, and there it was, her house, the one he had been to several times a week since as long as he could remember. It was set back from the main road, and much taller than that where he lived. It had white arched peaks at the front, and large windows in every room. It was a big place, four bedrooms, and clearly far too big for her, but she had been there near all her life and clearly loved it too much to leave, no matter what problems it offered.

Steven's mind focused on what to cook and how to prepare it, at least until he tripped, almost falling over himself. He stopped quickly, just in time to see Arthur stood before him, eyes bright, tail wagging, looking at him as if he was waiting for him to throw a ball.

Arthur stood, tremendously pleased with himself that he had enjoyed so much fun running around the great big bright place, and now all he wanted to do was go with his new friend as he showed him where home was.

"Now come on," Steven said irritably. "You need to go home."

The word *home* resonated with Arthur, being something that the lady he loved the most had often said. When they had gone on long walks in the summer sun, or short walks in the bitter winter, at the end she would always say 'Time to go home,' and off they went for treats, warmth and sleeping endlessly.

Steven and Arthur stood looking at each other, both a mirror of opposing thoughts. The last thing Steven wanted was to bring a stray dog back to his Gran's.

"Off you go now," Steven insisted, waving his arm out as if to say leave. Arthur misread it, thinking he had been thrown a ball and quickly ran out into the road, looking all around for the magic invisible thing. Steven figured all was well again, as his attempts to make the dog leave had worked, as it ran off again.

Relieved by his success, Steven walked to the small wooden gate, ready to turn in. As he did Arthur barged through, knocking the gate wide open, leaping off down the narrow concrete path.

Steven followed reluctantly, wondering how he was ever going to deal with the problem with four legs and a waggy tail.

Before he could say a word, the front door opened wide, spilling bright lights into the garden. Holding tightly to the door was his Gran, smiling as she looked out at him, expectant of her welcome visitor.

Arthur sprang up, running to the lady, thinking for a moment it was her, the lady, the one he loved more than anything or anyone else in the world. As soon as he got close enough, he knew it wasn't her, as difficult as it was to see for sure in the light, she certainly didn't have her lovely smell, the rosy perfume, the light air of lavender. Hers was all vanilla, and chocolate, which he knew wasn't allowed, but didn't really know why.

Arthur sat down, continuing to look at the woman expectantly. She was dressed in a baggy, worn sweater and plaid skirt right down to her scruffy slippers. Both continued to look each other up and down. Steven stopped before them, waiting for a reaction, anything to signal intent. He hoped she would have the experience and understanding of what to do, what the right thing might be to do.

"Steven," his Gran said. Steven stood to attention, waiting for her all decisive command.

"Yes, Gran," he replied, as expectant as any of them.

"You're not allowed dogs in the house, so he'll have to wait outside," she said, not unsurprisingly to him.

"Sorry, doggy, you have to go home again," Steven said, quietly slipped past him, through the door. He continued to looked at the cute little dog, wondering what it might be like to own a dog, but knowing nobody in his family would allow it. It was just one of those things. Perhaps when he was older he could choose for himself, but for now...

"Off you go," Gran insisted, again shooing her hand out. This time Arthur didn't fall for it, he knew it was a trick, there was no ball, they were still just playing games with him, but a different kind of one.

Without another word Gran turned her back to him, shuffled inside and closed the door. The lights went out, and once again Arthur was alone.

He continued to sit, waiting for the door to open again, for the light to come back and for the little old lady and the young man to come and help him find his home again. Nobody came. Minutes passed as he leaned his head, to the left, then to the right, trying to peer in, to see if he was missing something, if they were there really, and he was being too silly to notice.

Time passed, but nothing changed. Neither came back to him, and he was alone. As he wondered what to do, whether to howl a little or bark, deep down he refused to accept they had left him, on purpose, that it might be that he wasn't wanted.

His mind was made up for him as a small pat of rain hit him square on the center of his head. He shook a little, until another hit, and then another, lightly at first. Arthur had been out in the rain before, when the lady took him for walks and they got caught in the showers, it would be fun, because it was warm, and still he got to run for the ball and always but always went back home again. This time there would be no such thing, he was alone, properly alone for the first time in his life.

Finally, Arthur got the message, stood up and turned to walk out of the gate. He looked around, wondering which way to go, which way was home. He was a long way from there now, in the dark at night as rain began to pour all the heavier. Whichever he chose now, he began to understand, it was going to be a long, lonely night.

CHAPTER FIVE

That smell of chicken, it is so perfect, at least to a dog for sure. Or the smell of beef, or tuna, or any meat in fact. Chicken has always been Arthur's favorite, especially on a Sunday when the lady he loves puts on a full share of the regular potatoes, Yorkshire puddings, gravy and big pieces of freshly carved chicken. Like most such loved dogs, he is pampered and spoiled like a young child.

Arthur laps at the gravy, biting into succulent pieces of chicken and enjoying chewing on it. It must be a really special day, because there on the tile floor is another bowl, only it has large pieces of meat on the bone in it. Second only to chicken are bones, ones full of meat, which he can spend ages chewing on, cleaning his teeth and cracking open for their goodness inside.

Another pungent aroma catches his attention, something fishy. He knows cats all too well, fun to chase but impossible to catch. They smell fishy, but only because they eat so many of them. Still Arthur loves a nice a piece of tuna, and there is another bowl, full of thick chunks of tuna, smelling so wonderful.

A potato drops on the floor, still steaming hot, so he has to wait for it, then another drops, like the lovely lady always does, accidentally but on purpose. Arthur is never so rude that he sits and waits to be fed, he has been raised with much better manners than that, but it smells so gorgeous, fills his nose with scent, and looks so fluffy and soft that he can't decide which to have first.

Silly, of course he can decide, it's chicken, it's always chicken. Covered in tasty gravy. Arthur laps at it, nibbling bits of meat off. His tummy fills up and he knows just how lucky he is. He doesn't compare himself to other dogs, he doesn't have to, because he knows how lucky all dogs are, they all live such lives of luck and love.

Finally, unable to bear any more, so full he could burst, he walks a little, to the hugely soft, thick fleece he has on the kitchen floor. Of course he doesn't have to stay there, because he had another one in the living room, a different color, but the one in the kitchen is good for when it's too hot, and he is full, like every Sunday, when he empties that big bowl of food, the one with the pictures of happy dogs on it.

Arthur flops down onto the inviting fleece, nuzzles his wet nose into it, struggling to keep his eyes open. He is so full, so content, so warm and happy. It truly is a dog's life. Perfect. Forever.

CHAPTER SIX

"Move."

The sound seemed odd, not at all like Arthur was used to. Nobody ever spoke to him like that. His eyes remained tightly closed, accepting they must have meant someone else.

"Move," the voice barked ever louder. This time something nudged his tummy, but it wasn't a tickle, it was more than just a tap with something hard.

Voices continued muttering, sounding unhappy. Arthur opened his eyes, and all ideas of food and comfort melted away, as he could see in the daylight just where he had ended up. He could barely recollect how he had gotten to where he was, after so long wandering around. He was so cold and wet now as the rain poured heavier. He had hidden under a square box type vehicle with small round wheels. Directly in front of him were a pair of scruffy boots, in which stood a very tall man.

"Is it yours?" a voice asked.

"Not mine, never seen it before," another voice replied.

The scruffy boot shuffled a little closer to Arthur, lingering off the floor, near to his nose. Arthur lifted his head, looking at it warily.

"Out!" the voice connected to the man connected to the boot said. Arthur jumped.

"Out," the voice shouted again quickly, much louder. Arthur knew he had to move, so did slowly, pulling himself out, all the while keeping his eyes on the boot.

Finally he stood out, looking at the two men. The one with the boots was very tall, much more so than Arthur could ever recall seeing anyone before. He wore dirty blue jeans and a white sweater that had seen better days. Even his face was dirty, matching his hands, covered in oil and grease.

The man beside him looked much older with white hair, and was shorter. He too was covered in oil and grease.

As Arthur looked around, he noticed lots of cars, all broken and dented, looking as scruffy and dirty as each of the men.

"Go on, get out of here," the tall man demanded. Arthur stepped back.

"Ah Dad, a little doggy," a high-pitched voice offered. Out came running a young girl. In stark contrast to the men, she was spotlessly clean, wearing pigtails and a pretty dress, which looked as if it had never been near dirt, ever.

"Hold on, Alice," the white-haired man said, stepping between her and Arthur.

"Why? He's lovely," the girl insisted, beaming a loving smile at Arthur. He liked her; she was very friendly. He wondered if perhaps she might help him get home.

"He could have diseases," the tall man said, staring at Arthur.

"Really, Dad, how do you know that?" the girl asked, now standing with her hands on her hips.

"He could be ferocious," the white-haired man decided. Arthur decided to sit down, watching as the three battled it out.

"If he's ferocious, my name is Aunt Sally," the girl insisted. Not believing a word of it, she began to walk over to Arthur, hand out, ready to offer some love.

"Alice, don't you dare," a woman shouted, making them all jump.

Alice looked immediately round to see her mother approaching. She would argue all day with her dad and his mate, but nobody argued with Mum.

"But he's so nice," Alice pleaded.

"I don't care if he's a fluffy bunny wearing ribbons, we don't know him, and you're not allowed."

Alice burst out into mock tears, slapping her sides with her hands in a huff.

"That doesn't work on me. Come on, we're going to the shops," Mum ordered. Alice, head lowered, turned away from Arthur, waving gently as she shuffled away.

"As for you, off you go," Mum insisted, at which Arthur quickly stood up and began to walk away. He knew when he was beaten, he was quickly learning that much.

Alice watched him walk away, wishing she had a dog as lovely as he was. No one seemed to appreciate just how sweet he was, or how lost.

The streets around him were like some alien landscape, as if he had been plucked out of the beautiful fields and burrows of his life, and dropped into a concrete jungle, where everything either snarled at him, or threatened to make him dirty, cold or wet. For the first time in his life, he was having to learn more than just new ways to chew a bone.

Arthur knew one thing; he missed the lovely lady he had known all his life. She was all he could think of. Well, that and food! As he walked, he noticed how wet his coat had become, so shook it as much as he could, sending a spray out all around him. Much better, much, much better, dryer now. Within seconds he was all wet again. It seemed the more he walked, the more it rained, settling down on him as if he were a mop whose entire purpose was to soak up water.

"Oh, thank you," a lady offered. Her voice was light and polite, but as Arthur looked at her, she was holding a clear plastic umbrella, looking at him as if she were just a little angry. She slapped her light blue overcoat, as drips of water ran down it. It occurred to Arthur to wonder why, until it dawned on him that he had splashed her. If he could have apologized he would, but he didn't know how, other than to wag his tail or lick her hand, neither of which she seemed interested in.

The woman walked around him, giving him a wide berth, as if to suggest she didn't want to be near him. Normally when he met strangers, he was warm and dry, well fed and happy, and people who came into the house would immediately make a fuss of him, give him a quick hug, or say something that sounded happy and nice. Now everything was different, when they looked at him it was as if he wasn't wanted, or they appeared afraid of him. To Arthur it was a shock; how could anyone not love him anymore?

His paws felt unusually sore in a way that he had never experienced, the pads feeling every bit of ground, each little rock and pebble underfoot, every blade of grass. In all his life he could never remember walking so much. Even his back ached, which was newest of all. All he needed was a warm bed and all would be right again. Arthur was a plucky dog, strong willed and whatever happened would never, ever give up. He would walk on, and search and overcome, he would find what he was looking for come what may.

As he walked along something caught his attention. At first, he thought it was simply the flowers from the fields, but as he walked it grew stronger, no longer so delicate, as it filled his nostrils with a pungent smell of something he hadn't had in what seemed a lifetime.

Down the road stood a group of people of all types, a few younger, an older man, several others in smart clothes. Arthur felt wary, wondering what they might make of him appearing, as others had made it clear he wasn't as much loved as he had thought. Arthur learned quickly of just what a dog's life it was, good and bad.

He stood for a moment, watching on, trying to decide what to do. The rain finally stopped, allowing for a slight break in the clouds as a fine ray of sun broke across the ground around him, warming his fur. It felt such a stark change from how he had been only moments ago, to the point where he began to wonder if he was dreaming again.

He was brought fully down to Earth as the aroma made itself truly clear to him, and what it was, as a strong drift of it filled his senses. It was meat, sizzling hot meat, cooked and flavored, and all its smells and spices washed over him, as if he had been bathed in a liquid food hamper.

A large red truck stood at the end with a small group of people out front, all looking at it, some holding white paper with something in, some eating from them. Arthur felt curious, not just for the smells which were amazing to his keen sense of smell, but for what all the people were up to. For all his wariness, he couldn't resist having a closer look.

As he walked up, he noticed a woman, short and thin, dressed smartly, holding a white paper towel. In it appeared to be bread with a long thin piece of meat, covered in sauce. She kept biting at it, lapping up the neat sauce. Eat time she took a bite, Arthur did the same, instinctively opening his mouth, as if it were him taking the bite.

"Ha, hey, look at that dog, he's eating air," someone said. Arthur looked to see it was a young boy, his hair extremely short, wearing a striped t-shirt and baggy shorts. Stood next to him was a man dressed almost the same, as if they were short and tall twins.

The man looked at Arthur, watching for signs of him doing it. Arthur simply stood, looking at them both. Wondering what all the fuss was, the man took a large bite from a round bun with equally round meat on it. The moment he bit into it, Arthur did the same, opening his mouth wide, then biting down onto thin air. Both the man and the boy watched, catching him do it. The moment Arthur bit into nothing the man finally broke out laughing, dropping bits of bun and meat onto the floor, struggling not to choke on his food as he laughed.

"See, Dad, I told you, he's got his dinner and you can't see it," the boy insisted, giggling in between chewing his food. Unlike his dad, he wouldn't lose any of his food. If he did, he was never one to be picky, he would bend over, pick it up and stuff it in his mouth before anyone could object.

"Yeah, Simon, funny dog," the man replied.

"Dad, can I give him some of mine?" Simon asked, pulling a little of the bun off.

"No, hun, he might want more and then we'll never get rid of him." Simon didn't say a word about it, accepting it because it meant all the more for him. Besides, the dog didn't look so great, his coat all matted and dirty, and so wet, it wouldn't be a surprise if he had fleas. Yuck.

"Hey Joe, you have an audience." A woman said loudly, looking over to a man leaning from a window on the side of the red truck.

Joe leaned further out of the truck. He was a short man, hair thinning, wearing a stained, greasy, once-white apron. His hands were stubby but clean, and he had the looked of someone who loved his own food as much as others did.

"I guess so, no freebies though!" Joe exclaimed, his thick Yorkshire accent making it difficult for some to understand.

Simon looked up at Joe long enough to stop eating for a moment, not realizing he was staring. Joe caught sight of the look, feeling just uneasy, for a brief time. The boy hadn't mean anything by it, but he was curious, wondering how adults might treat the dog, where he would be happy to throw him something and even offer the dog a hug.

"You know, maybe he is hungry," Joe said, in such a manner which suggested he was proud of himself for being so kind. As if he were a missionary about to feed a starving village. All he needed was a round of applause and he would be ready to accept his humanitarian award.

The small crowd parted as Joe swung open his door and stepped off the burger truck. He waddled over towards Arthur, who quickly lifted up, beginning to wag his tail. He hadn't intended to, it was purely instinctive, having no choice over how it reacted.

Joe leaned over a little as he walked, holding out one hand, something in it wrapped in paper. Arthur couldn't help but feel better about things. Just as it all happened the sunshine broke through properly, as rays of warmth comforted him. For the first time since he had left his home, he felt happy again. Things would be alright.

Stood right in front of this little dog, Joe stopped and leaned over further, using his other hand to unwrap the paper. In the center of it was a mixture of bread and meat, none of it for people to eat, but for a hungry dog quite a feast.

"There you go young fella, check that out," Joe said, laying the paper on the floor in front of him.

Simon had continued to eat his burger, but stopped long enough to look up at his dad, a broad smile on his face, happy to see such kindness.

"Can I give him some of mine, Dad?" Simon asked.

"Nope," his dad replied succinctly, and that was that.

Arthur sniffed at the kind offering, not wanting to appear rude by not gulping it down, but being a dog, he was smart enough to check it out first, in case it wasn't actually food. Not only was it food, but it smelled amazing. Arthur finished his deliberations and licked the patty. It tasted spectacular, well-seasoned, perfectly greasy, and full of meat taste. It was tinged with a hint of tomato sauce and splatters of cheese. Without further ado Arthur took ahold of it with his mouth, biting chunks from it.

The sun shone, people were smiling at him and his mouth was full of tasty grub. Life had gone full circle, and he was once again the happy little dog that he had started out to be. The lady, the one woman he had known all his life, the one he missed the most, she would be proud of him, and pleased for him, wherever she was.

The last bits of bun and meat were the best, full of tasty grease and cheesy bits. Arthur looked up, licking his lips, his tail wagging furiously. Joe had begun to walk back to his van. Arthur looked on, hoping against hope that he would be back, perhaps with a bowl of water or even better, more food.

As Joe walked past, he smiled at the smartly dressed woman and patted Simon on the head. He stepped up into his van, walked round and closed the large flap to the side. Arthur watched, occasionally wagging his tail, occasionally sidestepping, as if to show he eager he was. A slip of black smoke jetted from the exhaust of the van as its engine fired up, and within seconds it began to drive away.

Arthur stood looking confused, wondering what had happened. One minute a kind man had fed him, the next he was gone. Perhaps someone else would take his place.

Simon looked at Arthur, seeing the reaction, feeling bad for what had happened.

"Come on, son, time to get going," his dad suggested, an arm around his son, before walking off. Others who had been in the group having finished their meals began to dissipate.

Simon looked at the dog, feeling down for him, wondering what might happen. In the end even he turned his back on Arthur, and in a few moments the little dog was alone again.

Feeling lost and alone once more, Arthur had no idea what to do. His hunger wasn't quite the issue anymore, and the sun held enough warmth that he no longer felt so tired or weary. Now though, he felt the isolation of loneliness, feeling that come what may in the future, his life would never quite be the same.

CHAPTER SEVEN

It was a long, long walk. It seemed as if that was all there was left to life, to walk endlessly. In the early days it would seem so to Arthur, but by the time he had finished his walking, it would be a lot of running, and then, well, life really did change.

For now, all Arthur could do was walk and search to find his way back, back to where he belonged. He walked past a park, which seemed nice, pleasant green fields, open and refined, but little shelter and nowhere to lay and hide. He continued, walking past houses, too tired to worry about what people thought, no longer quite caring so much if they walked away from him, even missing those who had a mind to help.

Eventually he turned a corner, not just in the street, but in life, as he came upon a large expanse of land, covered in debris-ridden gravel, beyond which lay a foreboding red building. It seemed large and oblong, covered in tall, white paneled windows, surrounded by swaying trees and tufts of grass here and there grown high and wild. It seemed empty and abandoned, long ago.

To the right lay a collapsed wooden shed, not much use for shelter, but certainly suggesting no one had been around in a long time. A small pathway led to the other side of the house, wending and weaving its way like a solid stream, leading off into nowhere.

Arthur looked on, and decided as tired as he was, going nowhere seemed just about right. He headed in.

Closer around the back of the huge red building it became darker, as bushes and undergrowth had grown out of control. It was obvious no one had been around to tend to it in such a long time that the house as it was had fallen into a state of disrepair. It was like an odd mixture of manmade and nature, where one had encroached on the other and the two were locked in a battle for who would win. Time was always the judge and in the end, there would only ever be one winner.

As he walked slowly through, Arthur thought how peaceful it was. In the past few days all he had known was excitement, worry and panic, not to mention all the emotion mixed with people around him being so fickle. Here however, in that moment of solitude he didn't mind being alone, because he could stop and think. He breathed in heavily, taking in lungs full of fragrant air, tinted with an easy blend of scented grass. Along the back wall were a full row of wild flowers, grown unchecked creating a vibrant array of vivid colors. To his eyes it was poor compared to how people might see it, but he still had the presence of mind to note all of its difference.

None of it was created by the hands of man, all of it unplanned and untamed. Between Arthur and the flowers lay a bed of grass, grown in every height and direction, pushed and pulled by the freedom to choose its own path. It seemed like a bed of nature which would offer the

perfect setting for sleep. It almost called to him, *come lay with me, feel the softness and splendor.* So he did.
*

The stark contrast when Arthur woke up to what he had closed his eyes to was immense, almost overwhelming. He had turned and laid in the center of the green, closed his eyes to images of color and warmth, only now to open his eyes to a tragic spray of powerful wind and rain. As he blinked, trying to take in what was going on, he noticed the skies were black, full of rolling clouds, as rain poured heavier and heavier onto him. Wind swirled around him like a tornado, tugging his fur in all directions, as his eyes struggled to cope with seeing anything in the onslaught.

Arthur quickly stood up, trying to keep his head as low as possible so that he wouldn't be buffeted by the high winds and rain. He began to shiver, as much from shock at what had happened as from being cold. All he could think of was one thing: go and find shelter. It was so dark he could hardly see, only able to perceive an outline of the large building nearby. He sprinted quickly over, doing his best not to fall. Just as he began to trot over a huge burst of light lit up the skies, followed by a shuddering thud as thunder rocked all around the place. It was as if the land and skies were at war with each other. Arthur felt terrified.

Another bright flash came, signifying another bone shaking thump, only this time Arthur caught sight of something reflecting him. As he neared, he could see the remnants of glass in a large oblong shaped window, long broken out, allowing access. Many of the windows were covered by boards, but this one had fallen away, now leaning against the damp yellow brick walls.

Without hesitation, Arthur was through the gap, just as rain driven ever harder by powerful winds tore around the place. Another shock of thunder burst around, terrifying Arthur in a way he could never have imagined possible.

Inside was even darker than out, but immediately the wind ceased and it was dry. What relentless rain there was got no further than a few feet into the building, forcing Arthur in. Once into the darkened room he stopped, before shaking for all he was worth. His coat splayed out, sending splashes of water away across the dusty walls.

The air in the room was musty, but he was thankful it was at least dry. Arthur stood and watched proceedings outside for a moment, trying to come to terms with what had happened. His heart beat hard in his chest, as he couldn't help but wonder if it all might spill inside.

In time he settled, accepting for now he was going to be safe from it all. As bad as it smelled, it was much preferable to what was going on outside. He wandered around a little, sniffing the floor, before sneezing with the dust. That was a bad idea. Feeling tired, he knew he had to sleep, so walked around a little, tried to find something suitable, and came across an old sheet. It had formerly been curtains, that had literally fallen from the window in disrepair and neglect, but it was better than a hard floor. Arthur tugged at it a little with his paw, then once again, before walking round in a circle, then again, and again in one last circle, before dropping down into a tight little bundle of damp fur. Sleep would never come easy again for him.

CHAPTER EIGHT

"Look over here, all these flowers," Samantha said. She was busy leaping over the tall grass, trying not to allow the bottom of her flowery cotton dress to get wet.

"Nah, I don't want flowers, yuck," Timothy replied. He was stumbling around the garden, in his super worn out black shoes, not the least interested if he got his too long black shorts wet, or if his equally flowery long-sleeved shirt got dirty. Why his mother hadn't given him a t-shirt to wear to play out he had no idea, but either way it wasn't going to be his problem.

"Let's go inside," Timothy called, but Samantha was busy, off picking a mixed bunch of yellow and red flowers, determined she would take them back for their mother.

"Come on Sam, come in," Timothy pleaded. He really wanted to go into the dilapidated old house, but given how dark it was inside, he was too afraid to go in by himself.

"I'm busy doing this."

"Aw Sam, come on," Timothy pleaded, determined to have his way.

"Help me do this first, and then once I have enough, I'll go with you." It wasn't ideal, having to pick flowers with his sister, but needs must. He stomped over to her, near the edge of the garden and stared at her, his face a picture of annoyance.

"Well, pick some," Samantha insisted. Hope that he might get away with just watching her do it disappeared, as he couldn't help but notice how much color there was in them. The rain from the night before was quickly evaporating, as the sun once again shone brightly, warming all around them. It was fast becoming a typically beautiful late summer's day, one memorable for many reasons to come.

Finally, Tim couldn't hold out any longer. It didn't seem the big boy thing to do, but it looked fun, and deep down he loved the thought of giving Mum a bunch of flowers. She might give him one of her super hugs, which he loved so much, but of course he wouldn't tell anyone that.

Wild seeds and flower elements pervaded the air, like frosty particles that never melted. White speckles floated around, sitting in the backdrop of an increasingly hazy day. It looked as if nature was exploding, all awash with color and movement, a truly spectacular and memorable day. One that they would both look back on with fondness.

"OK, that's enough," Samantha decided, standing up and wading back out from the waist high flowers.

"No, hold on, just a few more," Timothy insisted, as he jumped from one to the next, struggling to decide what to get, which looked better, which their mother might love the most. Samantha giggled loudly.

"What's so funny?" Tim asked, still picking diligently.

"Five minutes ago, you didn't want anything to do with flowers, and now here you are insisting you need more time to pick more." Samantha was aware that if she goaded him too much, he might have a fit of pique and throw the flowers, such was his young nature, but it was impossible to avoid how funny it was.

"Mum will like these," was all he said in response.

Samantha smiled. "Yeah, she will," she said quietly.

"OK, let's go have a look in the house, yeahhhhhh," Timothy said, so loudly and excitedly that he made his sister jump.

The two bounced through the long grass, over to the corner of the huge building. It looked so high to them it seemed as if it would go on forever, right up into the clouds. Paint flaked off the walls and windows were either boarded up or completely broken out, but to such young minds it seemed like a palace, a place where all their adventures and dreams could come true.

"Leave the flowers here, so they don't get damaged," Samantha said, placing her bunch on an old wooden case nearby. Timothy followed suit, only placing his well apart from hers. He didn't want his mixing up with hers, in case his mother thought hers were best even though he had picked them. Samantha noticed it, but smiled, remaining quiet.

Timothy peered inside, through a tall window, where only a wooden surround remained and glass had long since been removed. A large, flat wooden board lay on the floor, having been placed across the window to provide protection from entry, ravaged by time and neglect, fallen flat like a wooden carpet.

"It's dark in there," Timothy said warily.

"Smells funny too," Samantha agree, now leaning in beside him. "Maybe we should just go?" she asked, hopefully.

"Yeah, maybe," Timothy agreed, before stepping in, deciding as afraid as he felt, he couldn't resist having a look. He wondered what treasures might lie inside, as dark, smelly and empty as it clearly was.

"Tim," Samantha called, realizing she had no choice but to join him. She stepped in, her eyes struggling to adjust to the difference in light. Her brother was nowhere to be seen.

"Tim, where are you?" she called, wondering now if they might get into trouble if caught inside. As she finally grew accustomed to the place, she could see the difference from how it was and how it must have been. An old chair sat in the corner, round edges and plump upholstery. It was covered in thick layers of dust, but appeared in otherwise fine condition. It looked as if whoever had owned the place might once have sat there, and then just upped and left, and the chair sat waiting for someone to make use of it again, but never would. Curtains lay fallen across various high windows and doors and an old carpet lay square in the middle of the floor, worn by time and use so that its only pattern was that of its seams.

Samantha walked on a little, to a white door, half closed. She tried to move it, pulling it open a little wider that she might more easily move through, but it was stuck, collapsed from its hinges and now just leaning against the frame, as if it had breathed out one last, great sigh and given up forever.

The further in she went, the more acrid the smell. Damp permeated everywhere, but beyond the dust and neglect it was obvious how beautiful the place must once have been. A grand set of winding stairs led right up from the front doors, up to a landing area, which itself was far from safe. She determined they wouldn't go up there, ignoring the possibility that Timothy already had done.

Darkness wrapped itself around her like a dreary fog, making any sense of focus difficult. Samantha stood, looking as best she could, trying to ignore the scratching sounds she could hear.

"Come on, Timothy," she pleaded, almost under her breath for fear that she might alert something, anything.

"Hey," Timothy said loudly, as he walked out from a doorway at the side of the stairs. Samantha jumped so much she thought she might faint, as her heart pressed heavily and her mind lit up.

"Don't *do* that, Tim," she shouted, immediately regretting doing so.

"What?" Timothy asked innocently.

"Where have you been? We need to go," Samantha demanded, not caring what his answer might be.

"I was looking around, that's the kitchen through there," he said, pointing to the doorway. Beside it was another smaller door, leading directly under the stairs. It was almost too dark to see, but enough that they could see the door was slightly open.

"You should see it, it's amazing," Timothy said. His sister quite liked the idea of seeing a truly old kitchen, wondering what might be left of it, and whether there would be any utensils left, or anything worth seeing. She was torn, struggling to marry the ideas of intrigue and concern.

"OK, a quick look, then we have to go," Samantha insisted. Timothy smiled, but it was too dark to see. Together they walked slowly, heading back to the kitchen door.

Hidden, behind a wooden crate, laying in the darkness, amongst some old smelly blankets, was Arthur. He had wandered around the house, looking for somewhere that the wind and rain couldn't get him, eventually settling on a dry, dark place, where the choice was between a soft place to lay which was cold or somewhere smelly that was warm. He chose to put up with the smell, for the sake of getting away from the storm.

Although he desperately needed to go outside, he was afraid, wondering what it might be like out there, whether it was still stormy, but worse, the thought that if he went out, he might not be able to get back in.

For the first time since he had left the lady's house, he had felt safe. It didn't matter if he got a bit wet, because when she threw him a stick he would wade into the stream and bring it back, all soaking wet, but quickly shake and dry and run around, and soon he would be fine again. What mattered was what he couldn't see, what might occur, the possibility that he might never be loved again. That thought remained hidden in the back of his mind, wondering what to do next. The decision was made for him.

"It's awfully quiet in here," Timothy said, quietly in case he disturbed the peace the house was enjoying.

"Yes, it's so nice, I just wonder what this place must have been like so long ago," Samantha whispered, but she knew he wouldn't understand, being so young, so full of energy, he had little time to stop and wonder of life around himself in quite the way she did.

Arthur looked on, as confused and unsure of any of them. Usually when it was dark, he would bury his head in his blankets, keep his eyes closed and snore the night away. When he woke up it would always be to a kind smile and something tasty to eat. Now all he got were bad looks, something to eat if he was lucky, and wet and cold all the time. These two small people going past, he knew they were young, but what of them, would they be nice to him?

A minor rumbling broke the silence, followed by a deep, resonant growl. Arthur almost jumped out of his skin, wondering what it was, as both children froze, looking around themselves as if in fear that moving at all might shatter their worlds.

The rumbling growl continued, upsetting Samantha and Timothy, but frightening Arthur as much as anyone. He lay low, head to the ground, wondering where it was coming from. As it sounded, louder, deeper, it suddenly became clear, that he was the one growling, doing something he had never done before.

"What was that?" Samantha whispered, suddenly grabbing ahold of Timothy's shoulder.

"Dunno, I don't like it," Timothy replied nervously.

The two stood, looking around, wondering what to do. As they did, Samantha spotted something to the side of them, hidden in the darkness, two small round beads of light staring back at them. She froze, staring at them, unable to express herself in any way. Timothy was slow to respond, but eventually he plucked up the courage to look at what she was seeing.

"Agh, a monster!" Timothy screamed, not stuck like his sister. He jumped away, turned and ran outside. It was just what his sister needed, breaking the moment, as she too screamed, before turning to run back out. The tumult was too much, as Arthur jumped too, leaping up and out of his hideaway, scrambling around, trying to find safety, to get away from the growling dog, back to where he no longer felt afraid.

Timothy led, charging back where he had come from, bounding across the littered old living room, bursting through the broken window space out into the garden. Samantha ran behind, keeping a close eye on her brother, desperately wanting out. Just as she was about to make it to the window, a small brown dog jumped in front of her, headed right for the gap before leaping through.

Arthur ran past Timothy, into the center of the grass and stopped, quickly turning to look and see. He was terrified, wondering where the growling had come from. Timothy stopped dead, looking directly at him, as Samantha stood on the window gap, holding onto the frame like some intrepid explorer looking out to the scene of their latest adventure.

"Don't move, Tim, just stay where you are," Samantha called. It was the best she could come up with, beyond which she had no idea what to do. Timothy didn't need her orders, he had no intention of doing anything other than running again, in the opposite direction.

"I told you we shouldn't go in that house," Samantha pleaded.

"Oh, that's really helpful," Timothy shouted back.

Arthur lay slowly in the grass, heart pounding, breathing heavily, as he listened to sounds of growling, quieter but still present. He quickly looked around himself, trying to see where it was coming from, afraid that whatever it was would pounce on him any moment. Arthur was never the sharpest tool in the box, but eventually as he settled it became obvious, again, that the growling really was coming from him.. He was such a soft little dog, that even when someone knocked at the door and he naturally barked he was afraid of himself.

Timothy stood looking at Arthur as the little dog lay staring back at him. Samantha watched them both, wondering what to do.

"He doesn't look like a bad dog," Timothy said, maintaining eye contact with Arthur.

"No, that doesn't mean anything," Samantha insisted.

"So what do I do?"

"Just keep looking at him, and walk backwards slowly to me."

"Isn't that what you're supposed to do with bears, not dogs?" Timothy asked, feeling perplexed.

"Just do it," Samantha insisted.

Timothy made to step back from the crouched dog, but as he did Arthur shoved his bottom in the air and front paws down, head low to the ground. Arthur had no idea what he was doing, but it seemed like the right thing to do in the moment.

"Sam, what's he doing?" Timothy asked. Samantha didn't answer.

Arthur suddenly gave out a great loud yap, making himself jump as much as others. Just as Timothy was about to express his fear, Arthur leapt up and spun around in a full circle, before crouching again.

"Sam, what is he doing?" Timothy called, louder now.

Samantha stepped down from the house window, walking slowly towards her brother. As she did Arthur jumped up again, yapped once more and sprinted around the garden, bouncing over huge tufts of grass, then stopped, looking at them, crouched again. Even he was surprised by himself. He had always loved to run in a stream, and often loved running for a thrown stick, but the lady was never one to exert herself, or him, so anything instinctive or expressive was alien to him. Whatever it was, it seemed like the most natural fun.

"Sam, I think he's playing," Timothy suggested, still feeling wary of his intentions.

"Yeah, it seems like it, but you still never know."

The three stood, looking at one another, wondering what to do. Arthur felt all kinds of things, some that he never had before. He had seen children often, but never had much chance to engage with them. He wondered if they liked to fetch sticks and splash in streams. A sudden idea took hold of him, an urge which he couldn't resist. Suddenly, without warning, Arthur leapt at Timothy, charging towards him.

"Watch out," Samantha shouted.

Arthur jumped as the boy lifted his arms over his head to protect himself. He leapt, front paws knocking the boy over, before bounding away again, woofing lightly then crouching again. Arthur watched and waited for the response.

Timothy was flat on the ground, arms still covering his head, as he peered out from a gap, looking at the small dog, as he waited to play some more. He quickly sat up, breaking out into a huge smile.

"He does, he wants to play!" Timothy shouted, struggling to right himself. He jumped towards Arthur, arms out, suddenly without a care in the world.

"Tim, don't!" Samantha pleaded, but neither the dog or the boy heard a thing she said. Arthur leapt away, so quickly he almost fell over backwards. Timothy burst into loud laughter as Arthur responded with two fine and equally loud barks.

Samantha just watched at first, wondering what would be the best thing to do, what would be the most sensible. She shied away a little as Arthur ran up to her, stood in front and barked loudly twice.

"What, what do you want?" Samantha asked, hesitating.

"He wants to nibble on your leg," Timothy replied. Samantha wasn't at all amused. Arthur grew tired of waiting, yapped one more time and ran off, this time away round the back of the house, flying away so fast it seemed he had wings.

"Hey, hold on, wait," Timothy pleaded, acting as if Arthur would wait for anyone.

As Arthur ran, he began to feel different, no longer quite so afraid. He wasn't sure whether it was down to finally finding someone to be happy with, or something else. He flew around the corner of the house, away from the children, through some thick bushes, to a dark corner of the garden. He ran so fast he almost bumped into a large solid object right in front of him. He stopped, heart pounding, breathing heavily, mouth open, looking around, wondering what to do next. He looked up to see a large round object, colorful, looking like it had sat a long time.

"Hey, wait up," a voice called, as he could hear the children running closer. Arthur didn't mind waiting. He enjoyed a good run as much as anything, but the air was so warm and in the small close it was difficult to breathe. Pollen and dust swirled all around him as debris caught in the beams of sunlight cutting through the trees. It was peaceful, but deep down he wanted to run again.

"Hey, hold on, wait for me," Timothy insisted, springing through the undergrowth. He quickly ran over and knelt beside Arthur, his fearful caution long gone. Arthur sat easily, lapping up the attention as Timothy stroked his hand down the soft fur.

Samantha came upon them, bursting through the undergrowth like a wild thing, to see the two sitting next to each other. Arthur was loving it so much he was struggling to keep his eyes open. Timothy turned to look at his sister, smiling broadly, enjoying every minute of it.

"See, I told Mum we should get a dog, they're lovely," Timothy said quietly. Arthur was the perfect pet, just how he had always imagined a dog to be. Although this one seemed like he could do with a bath, as he was beginning to pong.

"We can take him home," Timothy decided.

"No, we can't just take him back, what if his owner comes looking for him?" Samantha asked, always the voice of reason. Secretly she would have loved to have a dog of their own, but for some reason she could never quite understand she couldn't quite bring herself to admit it.

"Oh, but he looks so lonely," Timothy pleaded. Arthur had remained sat, panting away, looking as if he didn't have a care in the world. Far from looking lonely, he looked more sleepy than anything else.

"Look, he's going to cry," Timothy continued, as Arthur finally succumbed to the urge and flopped down sideways. Just as Timothy was about to plead again, Arthur lurched over onto his back, flicked his tail once and drifted off into an easy restful sleep.

"Oh wow, a tractor," Timothy said loudly. Arthur thought about jumping up, but his body decided otherwise. It was too hot for such things, and he had had his fun. Timothy jumped up, looking directly ahead. Stood blocking the way was an old, rounded metal tractor, looking all of its age. Orange paint flaked off its sides and its tires were long collapsed, but the seat and steering wheel still held their position. It was too much to resist, as Timothy climbed on, ready to till the fields and plow the furrows.

"Tim, will you please be careful," Samantha insisted, stopping herself as she realized she was sounding what her mum called the *Mother Hen*, always fussing and never enjoying. As her brother played, she took a moment to look at the little dog, laid so quietly across the wild growth, surrounded by green growth and the vibrant Bluebells. He looked so at peace and happy. She knew Timothy was right, that he would be the perfect dog for them. She even dared to allow herself the thought that she could convince their mother as such.

"Come on, Timothy, we'd better get back," Samantha said. She knew what she was going to say next, just couldn't quite bring herself to utter the words.

Timothy looked straight at her, as if she had hit him with a verbal arrow. "What, no, what about the dog? We can't leave him," he said, his voice mirroring his feelings.

As awkward as it was between them sometimes, and as much as they argued, she loved her brother very much, and could never do anything to upset him.

"I tell you what, how about we leave him here, and go back and tell Mum about him, and if she thinks it's OK, we can come back and get him?" Samantha asked. As wary as she was, even she wanted to bring him home.

Timothy sat looking down at the ground, wondering what might happen.

"Can we drive this tractor back home then? If we can then that's fine?"

"Sure, if you can get it started," Samantha replied. She was used to her brother's antics, always ready for a quick reply.

"OK," Timothy said, suddenly pretending to flick a switch. He burst out making loud rumbling noises, swaying sideways as if the thing were up and running. "Hop aboard," Timothy shouted, interrupting himself. Samantha laughed, pleased he was in such good spirits. She walked over and climbed up next to him, enjoying the moment.

Arthur continued to lay, soaking up the sun which had finally filtered through the high trees, warming his fur. He kept his eyes open, watching as the young girl had walked past, climbing up onto the huge thing that had blocked his path. He watched quietly, not daring to move, not wanting to spoil the moment, as the two children sat beside one another, laughing and giggling, playing their own little games. He had no clue what they were doing, but it seemed so sweet, so loving, just what he wanted most of all.

"OK, come on, let's go. Tell Mum about the doggy, and see what she says," Samantha suggested, timing it just right so that her brother would be in a good enough mood to want to leave without the dog.

"Alright, if you say so," Timothy replied, aware of how sullen he was sounding, but as happy as he was, he couldn't shake the thought that they might not come back.

Arthur turned to his side and lifted his head as the two stepped down and began to walk away. They wouldn't leave, not now, not after so much fun, would they? He tilted his head to one side, confused by it all. Timothy turned to look back, staring at Arthur as he went.

"It's OK boy, we'll be back soon," he said. He stopped a moment to point his finger towards the dog. "Stay, stay there," Timothy demanded, hopeful that the dog would listen. He seemed such an intelligent animal, surely he would do as he was told.

"He's clever," Samantha offer, smiling at her brother as they walked.

"He is, isn't he?" Timothy replied.

"I think Mum will like him," Samantha agreed, feeling happy about things.

"Yeah, come on," Timothy said, his face a picture of happiness as he took her hand and broke out into a smile. They picked up the waiting flowers and walked off.

Arthur finally sat up, watching them go, his little tail wagging. He wondered if they were going to hide from him, to play a game. He waited a few moments, then a little longer, but with each passing minute, his tail wagged just a little less. Eventually he was surrounded by birdsong and the rush of the fine summer's air around him, but otherwise, he was alone again.

*

"Mum!" Timothy shouted, running in to the house so fast the door swung into the wall.

"Tim, be careful please," his mother insisted. She was sat in a comfy chair in the corner of the lounge, quite happy to relax until tea time. She was knitting, while watching her favorite program on television, The Jeremy Kyle Show.

"Mum," Timothy said again, as much as he could pronounce, given how out of breath he was.

"Oh Tim," his mother continued.

"What's he's trying to say is, when we were out playing, we found a stray dog, and he looked all frightened and alone, and he wants to know if you will come and look at it?" Samantha said, all calm and collected.

"What? No."

"What? Mum!" Timothy shouted, struggling not to burst into tears.

"It's OK Mum, he's a lovely little dog, so cute and friendly," Samantha offered, remaining as calm as ever.

"I'm watching my programs," their mother insisted, as both looked at her as if she were daft.

"Please Mum, you'll see he's really lovely."

"What if he belongs to someone?"

"He doesn't have a collar on, and looks like he had been staying in the house quite a while. He looks hungry too," Samantha continued, becoming aware that she was sounding as in need as her brother.

"Which house?"

"The old manor house," Timothy offered as Samantha cringed. She knew what the reaction would be.

"Er, haven't I told you not to go in there?" Their mother asked, sitting forward.

"No," Timothy replied immediately, knowing full well otherwise.

"It's nice there," Samantha explained, the happy look on her face offering some kind of reassurance about how sensible both were anyway.

"Oh alright, I'll have to get something suitable on," their mother insisted, struggling to stand up. She was dressing in a light cotton pant suit, with fluffy black slippers on her feet.

"You're fine," both children stated loudly at the same time. The three looked at each other, shocked, each waiting for someone to say something, but nobody did.

Together they left the house and began walking.

"Isn't there anyone at that old place, at all?" Mother asked.

"Nope, nobody but a little doggy," Timothy said, excitement evident in his voice.

"It's such a shame, so beautiful. I wish we could live there," Samantha offered.

"Of course, then all it needs is huge amounts of money to fix it up," mother replied.

"Can we?" Timothy jumped in, giving his mother such a look that she wondered if he was actually serious. Samantha laughed at them.

The walk was long and pleasant, filled with happiness and excitement. Timothy wondered what it might be like to get their own dog, and all the things they would do together. He could throw toys for him, and get him a bone and lay with him and all sorts. Samantha wondered if he would stay, or be allowed, but deep down hoped so, that it would another welcome member of the family. Their mother had her mind on dog food, bathing it, vacuuming fur endlessly, and nonstop barking!

"Right, where is he then?" Mother asked as they walked through the wide-open gates towards the house.

"He's in the back, in the garden hidden in the grass," Timothy said, breaking off into a run.

"Be careful," their mother shouted.

"He might be back in the house, you'll have to call him," Samantha shouted to her brother.

As Samantha and her mother walked around to the side of the house, they both come upon Timothy, stood talking to a man. The man was wearing a brightly colored jacket and a heavy plastic helmet on his head.

"Mum," Timothy said, his voice shaken.

"Hi, is the dog yours then?" their mother asked.

"No," the man stated, his voice deep, his accent pure Northern England. "There was a dog here, but when I came in, I started blocking up the windows and he barked and ran off," the man continued.

"Oh no," Samantha said, her voice matching her brother's.

"What are you doing with the place, knocking it down?" their mother asked, aware of the depth of feelings between them all.

"No, boarded up to keep people out, but it's going to be renovated soon, so they want it protected," the man explained.

Timothy ran away from the group, towards the garden. "Here boy, here you are, we're back," he shouted, clapping his hands.

"Was he your dog?" the man asked.

"No, he seemed like a stray, we were thinking of providing a home for him," Samantha explained. She had a look of sadness about her which she tried to mask. The last thing she wanted to do was make things worse for Timothy.

"Oh, I'm sorry, like I said to the young boy, when I began hammering these boards up that little dog just ran a bit. He stopped and looked again, and then just shot away out of the front. I've no idea where he went, I'm sorry."

"Oh, what a shame," Mother said, looking from Samantha to Timothy.

Hearts sank all round. Timothy looked crestfallen, his arms limp by his side, head down as if it weighed all of the world. He walked slowly back to his mother, falling into her arms, bursting into tears. Samantha couldn't help herself, putting her arm around her brother and following suit. The three stood for a moment, holding each other, heartbroken that Arthur was gone, and their dreams of having a dog of their own dashed.

Arthur was indeed gone, off again running, alone and afraid, still looking for someone to love him.

CHAPTER NINE

"Hey, get away," a voice snarled. Arthur looked up, to see a burly man in a colorful jacket and a strange hat looking at him. From the sound of his voice and his appearance, he wasn't likely to be very friendly. Arthur remained wary, one front paw off the ground, as if to say he was ready for him. He stood, staring at the man, as a haze of late summer heat beat around him and particles of pollen filled the air. It was an otherwise sublime summer's day, perfectly sunny and so peaceful, all he had wanted to do was sleep. That wasn't going to happen now.

"Go on, off you go," the man said again, moving slowly towards him. Arthur watched, wondering if as he got closer, he might kneel down and give him a hug. It was what people usually did when they saw him, always finding him to be so cute and loving.

The man walked halfway across the tall grass, before leaning over and picking something up. Arthur didn't blink, as he noticed the man had taken hold of a short, thick stick, holding it up. He had been right, the man wanted to play, he was ready for fun. Perfect.

"Move," the man said again, his voice deeper, looking at Arthur any way but playfully. He lifted his hand higher, before launching the stick. Arthur watched, as it sailed off in the air, watching for where it would land so he could go and fetch it. It took him completely by surprise as the heavy stick cracked him on the head. Arthur winced, feeling pain, wondering why the man had been so silly, throwing it that badly.

"Go on," the man said again, only now louder. He leaned over again, his tubby belly dropping out over his jeans, making his movement slow and lumbering. Still he managed to find another stick. He stood, then threw it again, straight at Arthur, only this time he was prepared, jumping out of the way. As a loved dog in the past, he was slow to react, always trusting and affectionate, but slowly it was beginning to sink in. Life it seemed, wasn't always perfect, and neither were people.

Even after the second stick flew past his head, Arthur's tail wagged, his ears remained up, his tongue out as he panted, waiting expectantly for some fun, a sign that he was wrong and the man was simply being foolish.

"I said go," the man shouted, now lumbering heavily towards him. Arthur jerked back, a little shocked by his sudden reaction, but stopped again, eyes wide, looking to see if he had still made a mistake. As the man got right to him, he swung out a big boot, swinging around to catch Arthur, but as trusting and hopeful as he was, he was no fool. Arthur jumped right out of the way, avoiding the flying boot. The man swung too hard, his leg twisting him and turning, as the expectant thud failed, forcing him to swing too far. Like an elephant ballerina the man twisted and turned, completely out of control, before his other leg gave way, sending him crashing to the ground like a great fat house brick. Arthur stood away, his tail wagged once, with one last vestige of hope that it was all a game, fading away, to the realization that not everyone loved him. Memories of the lady, the one who raised him and protected him so much began to fade.

Arthur was simply unlucky, bumping into one of the few, rare people who didn't love dogs. He was a jobsworth, out to do as he pleased, ignoring the plight of a lost and lonely little dog. The kind doggy wouldn't pass judgement on everyone because of the action of one small minded little man, but from that moment on, he would never be quite so innocent again.

All thoughts of waiting for Timothy and Samantha vanished, as he accepted the need to move on. Besides, his tummy was rumbling, and after so much effort, he was thirsty too. The last thing he saw as he trotted out of the gate was the man on his hands and knees, struggling to get up, returning a furious look. Arthur ignored it, setting off for yet another adventure.

*

The road outside the manor house was busy, two lanes of black tarmac either side of a grass verge, with cars racing up and down so fast it was impossible to see inside. The sun was at its hottest, and all Arthur could think of was to get away, to get a drink.

Up and down as far as he could see from the house was a long winding road with fields on all sides. Further down, in the distance he could see large buildings, and knew all too well, with buildings came people. He was torn- should he go in search of food and drink there, or should he stay away from yet more problems. As he stood looking out, his tummy rumbled so loud he thought the ground was shaking. His mind was made up.

The biggest problem was it was all on the other side of the road. Arthur looked up along it, seeing one car rush past so fast it was a blur, then another, and another, so many he wondered if they were all connected. He stood panting, even heavier, as the sun baked the fur on his back. It was a terrible predicament for him, one where his need outweighed the risk, but for the first time in his life he had to make a stark choice. Either way had the potential to be painful.

Suddenly there was a gap, no cars. Arthur leapt quickly out into the road, stopping just as quickly as a deafening blare of a car horn screeched at him, demanding he stop and look. He stopped, then tried to move, as another car came speeding up at him, this time slamming on brakes, skidding near to him. Arthur just went for it, as more horns blared, beeping repeatedly, engines revving. The fur on his back lifted up, as if he were preparing to fight, his ears lowered, eyes beady, ready to be hit and hurt any second. He just continued, ignoring the loud chants and sirens, jumping onto the grass verge.

"Stupid dog," someone shouted through an open side window, as cars once again sped up to leave. More horns sounded, making Arthur cower.

Now he was stuck, as cars rushed on both sides, faster and faster, so many of them, it seemed as if in reality they were circling him like angry buzzards, wanting a piece of him, and if not, an excuse to rage towards him.

As he stood looking out towards the large buildings down the road, he wondered if this was it, stuck there forever. He kept feeling an urge to just go for it, to trust he would be alright. It was usually the way to be, that life was good and no one would ever harm him. Before he would have done it, but now, a little nagging instinctive voice inside his head told him not to. If not, then what?

As he looked on, down the road a little, he watched car after car go past, until for no particular reason, a small red car slowed, then stopped, right before him. Inside was a woman, someone with white hair and a kind smile, much like the lady who had loved him all his life. In his dreams, in his hopes it would be her, come to rescue him, but she remained, smiling at him, waiting, as another car beside her suddenly slowed, stopping in its lane beside her. Inside was a man, this one younger, as deafening music bounced out of the part open windows. The two cars stopped, waiting, as if time had stopped, to allow this poor little dog find its freedom.

Arthur felt hesitant, but it was now or never, so ran across the road, still thinking and feeling inside that something bad was going to happen. It never did. He got to the other side of the road and continued trotting away, down the hill, not daring to look back, not wanting to see anything bad, but missing the kindness that had been shown to him.

The young man, bouncing to his music looked at the lady in the car opposite and smiled, as she looked to him the same. It was a minor thing, but good things often lead to better things in life, and rarely cost anything. So why not? Both drove away, as the little dog once again went safely on his way.

*

The roads around Walton often become busy, in small part because of the people who live in the houses there, and because of a great, huge, ancient-looking pub on the corner, which should attract far greater attention than it does, simply because it looks amazing. Everywhere around the area is at least pretty, ignoring the great slab of black line tar which dissects it, ruining what nature intended.

Small roads lead into the area, one past houses, sitting and looking as if they wished to be ignored. Of course, all that ever gets ignored is the desire not to be noticed. A second road goes up to a canal, and a myriad of trees, and a small church nestling so cozily that it might be hidden for all but believers. Further along is a place for the many cars that house all the people that endlessly visit there, and then on the opposite side, over an old brick bridge is Walton Gardens, a house in the middle for old times, surrounded by majestic beauty for all to see. Which they do!

Arthur wanted to see as much as anyone, in eternal hope that his needs might be fulfilled, and that he could go and have a lie down after. Walking wasn't such a problem, except when it didn't involve walking to and from a place of fun. As he approached the traffic lights, which bridge all of the roads in the small area, he could see many more cars ferrying people to and fro, mostly fro, into the place he had never seen, but would come to remember forever.

As he slowed his walk along the narrowing tree-lined path, he came upon various people, all doing the same as he, heading up in the same direction. Some were women, holding the hands of children, others were small boys on bikes with older men on bikes, mostly wearing helmets and riding along, merrily enjoying their day. It was a picture of color and vibrance, so much happiness that even to him it was a joy to behold.

Out of the corner of his eye he spotted some children, congregating on the opposite side of the road. He crossed over, it being a smaller road, with less cars, travelling slower due to all the people, and not for the first time or the last in his life, he got lucky. As he approached the group, he could see them stood before a long wooden table, with colorful plants in rows across the top. Arthur stopped, looking up, but he was so small his nose barely poked above the edge of the table. The group of children looked at him, wondering what he was going to do, but all that happened was a little shiny black nose bobbed up and down as its owner sniffed.

A giggling noise stopped him from sniffing, and he peered under the table to see where it was coming from. A small girl stood the opposite side, leaning underneath, trying to see him. She had long curls which fell across her shoulders, almost cutting off her view of the odd dog that seemed interested in buying their plants. She giggled as she looked at him, feeling how funny it was to see a dog out shopping.

"Julie, stand up, in case someone wants to buy something."

Julie looked up to see her older brother staring down at her. He wasn't much older than her, but had grown so tall he seemed more like a huge tree than a person anymore. She half expected branches to grow from him and leaves to bloom, so that small birds might sit on his shoulders and sing to the skies.

Arthur sat, waiting to see if anyone noticed him again, or did anything worth waiting for. Nobody did. All he could see were a row of legs, different sizes, some in socks, some bare, one in wellington boots, all stood as if to attention. As he waited, people walked past, moving around him, stepping part on the road to avoid him. Everyone seemed so polite, that they might chance upon a meeting with car, just so that he could remain there, being ignored.

After a few moments he stood up again, wagging his tail as if that might get him noticed, but stopped when it didn't. Once again he sat. More in hope than anything else he peered back under the table, to see the little girl bent over, staring at him. His ears pricked up, as if he had been mock surprised over it, making her giggle.

"Stand up," a hushed voice urged the girl. She remained bent over, so low that her face mirrored the too-big wellington boots she wore. It was a sunny, warm day with little chance of rain, but Sandra loved her wellies and there was no way she was taking them off, and that was that.

"He's still here," Sandra said harshly, trying to whisper like her big brother, but instead sounding like she had a sore throat.

"Ignore him," her brother insisted, but it was difficult, when the dog kept staring at her, and besides, he was so cute.

"James," Sandra said, tugging at her brother's shirt. James ignored her, looking ahead as if it were the right thing to do, that dogs would immediately leave if you ignored them. Besides, he was there to sell plants, and one day wanted to be a shopkeeper, so he had to look his best.

"James," Sandra said louder, tugging his shirt so hard it lifted from being tucked into his trousers. Finally, that worked.

"Sandra, if we don't ignore it, it'll follow us when we go in," he insisted, as if that might be some kind of deterrent against his sister doing it more.

The idea suddenly appealed to her, as her mind lit up at the thought of a new pet, one that would go nicely with their parrot, the frogs in the pond and the lump of wood she called Charles, but which was actually a garden ornament.

"Hey boy, what's your name?" Sandra called. She wiped her long curly hair from her face, to see Arthur had stood up again and was wagging his tail once more. The moment was perfect, as each looked at the other, she smiling, him wagging his tail in pure happiness that someone had finally noticed him.

"Sandra," her brother said loudly, making the other two children beside them jump. Everyone looked at her, then to Arthur, wondering what was going to happen.

It was wonderful, as he had gone from two children he had loved, to more who loved him as much. It was all too much to bear, too much to resist, so he didn't. Arthur jumped up, front paws onto the rickety table, as plants in pots and tubs shook and moved.

"Careful," James shouted, trying to hold onto the table. His young friend Billy, stood beside him stepped back, all wide eyed and afraid, wondering who the attack dog was, and wanting the toilet for the tenth time of the day.

Sandra stood back, giggled louder than ever at Arthur's antics, and began to clap loudly. "Go doggy," she shouted.

"I'm telling..." the fourth and final of the group said, an older girl, sister of Billy and occasional girlfriend of James. She was twelve years old going on forty.

"What? No..." James spluttered, trying to reassure her and hold onto the table at the same time. He was only eleven himself, but often had trouble walking at the same time as thinking, let alone dealing with dogs, tables and annoying children.

Arthur barked, his way of saying hello, but to others it seemed a little like a threat. Sandra suddenly changed her expression, wondering if he was so cuddly and soft after all. She stepped back, once again tugging at her brother's shirt, as if it was a hidden form of communication, designed to deal with any eventuality without the need for words.

Nobody did anything else after Arthur barked, all looking at him. To him it was an invitation for more, so he did, barking three times, once more for hello, once for how are you and the other for *I'm thirsty!* All together they hushed, stepping back, each holding onto the other.

As the group moved away, Arthur took it as a sign to play, so front paws on the table, he tried jumping with his back legs a little, to show he was ready to play. His tail wagged so hard everything shook.

"Good doggy," Sandra said, meaning well, but being too young to read the situation, she had no idea what would happen next.

To Arthur, it was the perfect invitation, a most happy welcome. One, two, then three he leapt up, fully onto the table, panting away in the hot sun, needing a drink, wondering why all the plants were getting in his way.

"No," James shouted, as Sandra laughed out loud. Billy stood, arms folded, looking annoyed, figuring they wouldn't be making enough money from selling things to buy an ice cream after all.

"I'm going in," Billy's sister said, turning in a huff, not before giving James a dodgy look, as if it were all his fault.

"But..." James tried to say, surrounded by pandemonium.

Arthur barked once, more, looking directly at Sandra, as she lost control of her laughing, tears in her eyes, giggling away merrily to herself. The excitement was too much, as Arthur jumped up and down on the table, enjoying every moment of it. Next up they would go into the house and he would get a drink and some food, and maybe even a hug.

As he was lost in his dreams, wondering how comfy the sofa might be, he suddenly felt a shove in his side. As he looked, he could see James, pushing him away, trying to get him off the table before stepping quickly back in case Arthur didn't like it.

Far from it, Arthur took it as a sign of being playful, and dropped down onto his haunches, front paws bowed, eyes eager, waiting for another sign to play.

By now a crowd had begun to assemble, not to see plants, but to witness all the commotion.

James knew he had to do something, because clearly the dog wanted to play, which was fine, just not on his mum's decorating table, and certainly not with all the plants on there that his dad had spent ages growing for them.

"Good doggy," James said, copying his sister's actions, without even thinking about it.

That was it, the trigger, ready to go. Arthur yapped once, then spun around on the table, knocking plants off here and there, before jumping up a little, scurrying to the end of the table and back again.

"Noooo," James shouted.

"Yeeees," Sandra shouted back in between bursts of laughter.

Arthur lapped it up, leaping from one end of the table to the other, as Sandra laughed and James watched on in horror.

"What is going on?" a louder, deep voice demanded. Everyone looked to see a tall, thin man walking out from the house. Even Arthur stopped, mid run, mouth open, eyes on the man, wondering who had done what.

"It's this dog," James began to say.

"He's so funny," Sandra said, giggling some more.

"Off," the loud voice shouted, as Arthur continued to stare at him. He could tell something was off, different, but wasn't sure if this was still part of the fun.

"Go," the man said, now standing beside the table. He had no hesitation, as he leaned over, placed a firm hand on Arthur's side and pushed. Arthur lost balance, as the slippery surface proved impossible to stand on. Before he could fall sideways, Arthur leapt up, into the crowd of people, throwing himself like an acrobat towards the road. The table gave up, following his lead in the opposite direction, hurtling towards the ground, as plants soared and pots scattered, soil all over, with a big crash it landed making everyone jump.

Arthur landed deftly with his front paws just as a car approached, its horn blaring out. He jumped instinctively back and away, turning to see the shouting man approaching him, as others moved away from the tumult.

All the while Sandra laughed, her eyes lit up with joy and happiness. She could tell he was a wonderful dog, so loving and playful. What she would do for such a pet as he. Of course it would never happen, whether due to her brother's fear, or her dad's annoyance, Arthur would never be welcome. As much as she laughed and enjoyed it all, she knew that.

Arthur looked at her one last time, making eye contact with her. She did the same, and for a moment the laughter died, as the two looked at one another, knowing. Full of love and happiness, it was a last goodbye, and they would never see each other again.

Years later and much older, Sandra would look back on the moment and still laugh, that funny little brown dog, the one that liked to dance on tables. She would always wonder what happened to him.

CHAPTER TEN

"Alice, push that buggy a little closer," Marina said. Alice stood up reluctantly, wanting to do nothing more than lay in the sun and text on her mobile phone. She didn't even have the energy to argue about it.

"Jack, get the bags, we'll have something to eat," Marina continued, as she nudged the light cotton umbrella further across six month old Jessie. The sun was hot, almost unbearable, and the last thing she wanted was her young baby to get burnt by it all. It was nice being out, as long as everyone helped, and everyone got along, a rare thing indeed.

"What's for tea, Mum?" Jack asked, eyeing the large, light green cool bag under the pushchair.

"It's not tea, dummy," Alice insisted, barely stopping texting long enough to reply.

"Don't talk to your brother like that," Marina replied, looking straight at her. "But no, it's not tea."

"See, Mum agreed with me," Alice poked.

"Yes, I did, but."

"That you're a dummy," Alice said quickly, before her mother could finish her sentence.

"Mum," Jack said, seeking sympathy. Marina looked at them both, feeling the hot sun through the fine white cotton hat she wore. It was going to be a long day.

Before anything more could be said, Marina pulled at the large picnic bag, unzipped it and began foraging around inside. She knew that would work, that would take their minds off each other, even if it was for just five minutes.

"Cheese sandwiches for you," Marina said, handing a sliced white sandwich to Jack.

"Tuna for you," she said, handing it to Alice.

"Bottle of milk for you," she said, lifting up a baby bottle and placing it gently in baby Jessie's demanding hands.

"Finally, mine," Marina said, lifting out a clear plastic tub of fresh salad.

"Where's mine?" Jack asked mid munch on his sandwich. He stared at her, mouth unmoving, looking at her as if to accuse her.

"Hey, I like that," Alice insisted.

"It's got egg in it, you don't like egg," Marina replied, looking directly at Alice.

"I do now," she replied simply.

Marina gave up, too hot and tired to deal with it all. The last thing she needed was an argument over silly salad, even though she was really looking forward to it.

"Here," she said, dumping it onto the large plaid wool blanket they all shared. Like gannets the two grabbed at it, emptying its contents.

Just as the bowl was all but empty, Alice looked at her mother. "Yuck, it's got eggs in it, I don't like eggs," she said, still chewing on the food. Marina looked at her, lost, wondering what she had to do to get fair treatment.

It had seemed like a good idea at the time, lovely weather, eating a picnic, enjoying family company. Reality of course was always different, but for the sake of the love of her children, Marina would carry on, and no doubt they would look back on it with better memories than it actually deserved.

"Would anyone like a drink of pop?" Marina asked chirpily.

"Yes please," Jack demanded.

"Oh yeah, please," Alice replied eagerly. Marina smiled. She would be content with two things, one that something made them happy, and second that both had said please. She was doing something right after all.

As she poured fizzy pop into a plastic beaker, a loud commotion in the distance distracted her, long enough so that as she poured her hand wandered, allowing fluids to drop all over the clean blanket.

"Mum, watch out," Alice said, herself just as distracted.

Marina lifted the bottle up, then continued to look in the distance, as another group sat eating all sprang up or rolled away. Whatever the fuss, it was attracting plenty of attention. Amidst the cries and laughter, sounds of shouting and yelling, she could just about make out something moving around in circles, creating an almighty fuss.

"What is that?" Jack asked, staring hard at the madness beyond.

"No idea, love," Marina replied, wondering if wasps were invading the jam, or like her someone had spilled something.

"Probably an angry moose," Alice said, intentionally being silly, quite aggrieved when no one laughed at her minor joke.

Marina squinted, trying to see what it was. As she was about to give it up and ignore it, back to her own problems and family, she noticed something bouncing up and down. It wasn't far away but her sight wasn't the best. She looked over at Jack, who likewise was staring, only he had a great grin on his face. Alice was too busy back on her phone to notice or care, but it seemed odd. As she looked on, she could see something shiny and black, behind which were two eyes, looking at her, as its head bobbed up and down.

"That's funny," Marina said, at which Jack nodded, smiling, ready to laugh about it.

"What is, Mum?" Alice asked, her head buried in an Instagram post from someone she barely knew.

Before Marina could respond, she jumped up and Jack followed suit. The bouncing nose and eyes rapidly became a bounding body, as Arthur, having the fun of his life came charging at them, heading for more antics with people who clearly wanted to join in. Alice never even had time to look up as Arthur crashed headlong into her, knocking her flying, sending her phone up in the air like a kite on a beach. Alice barely noticed the little brown dog as it knocked her over, her attention was simply fixed on the flying phone, and how that she might retrieve it to finish her response.

Arthur stopped long enough to see the plastic bowl, with remnants of egg and salad. The other picnic had been good, little nuggets and morsels here and there, but every time he had tried to nibble on something it had been snatched away. They were simply too quick for him, which while fun didn't exactly fill the tummy.

Arthur lapped at the snack, flicking bits of lettuce here and there, which he wasn't too keen on, but beggars couldn't be choosers, so in it went.

"Stop," Marina shouted, pulling Jessie's buggy away.

"Food!" Jack shouted, all wide eyed and loving it.

"Muuuuum," Alice called, the ubiquitous call whenever something in her teenage life went wrong. Her phone had plonked back down gracefully on the soft blanket, but she couldn't reach it because a small dog was hopping around on it, sniffing for all he was worth.

Jack quickly bent over, grabbed a packet of crisps, split them open and began sprinkling them on the ground like confetti, laughing to himself, ignoring the consequences. Arthur's eyes lit up, as did his nose at the smell of fresh salt and vinegar. Immediately an image flashed in his mind of sitting beside the lovely lady, so quiet and prim, as she delicately opened a packet of such crisps, and would munch away on them, thoughtfully dropping one for him every now and then. It reminded him how much he missed her, that beautiful face, her glittering eyes which always smiled when she looked at him. How much would he give to be back with her now? All the crisps in the world probably, but deep down he was realizing perhaps no more.

Finally, Arthur stopped his antics long enough to look up at the people around him. Marina looked at him as if he were a wild lion wanting to go and eat her children. Jack looked at him as if he were his own personal pet and plaything, someone to get up to all sorts of mischief with. Alice didn't look at all, she had dropped to her hands and knees and was trying to sneak up on him to grab her phone. Her ruse failed, as Arthur spotted her. Instinctively he did the only thing any dog would do in such circumstances, he leapt at her, licking her face repeatedly, slobbering her with what drool he had. Given the heat of the day, and all the food, he was parched; it was the best he could do.

"Here boy, crisps," Jack said, pointing to the scattering of food.

"Jack, don't, he might try to eat you," Marina said, in all seriousness. Jack burst out laughing, more for his mother than the antics of the weird but fun dog. Arthur just stood looking at them both, wondering which was going to get him a drink.

"Here," Jack said, picking up a crisp, holding it to Arthur's mouth. Arthur ignored it; he was far too thirsty for such salty things now.

Before anyone could say another word, Arthur sprang away, leaping and bounding along like a newborn puppy. The park was full of families and people milling around, and more fun than he could ever remember having. As he ran away Alice grabbed her phone, looking at it horrified.

"What's up, did he break it?" Marina asked fearfully.

"No, he got a muddy paw on it," Alice cried, as if her illusionary world inside metal and glass had been stained forever.

The three of them and baby Jessie watched as the crazy dog went off on his adventures. They wouldn't forget him in a hurry, he wouldn't let them.

Drink, water, puddles, anything, that's what Arthur needed. Even a dropped ice cream would do. As he trotted along, he had necessarily slowed due to the heat and his dryness. His mouth hung open, tongue dropping out like a flaccid, flat sausage. Something had to be done, quickly.

As he looked around, families jumped up and away, trying to avoid their food and picnics being spoiled by an overly eager dog. Children looked on in awe as parents ran around grabbing things. Arthur was oblivious to it all, he just needed a drink.

Something shiny in the corner of his eye caught his attention, glittering and suggestive of what he wanted. Without a better option, Arthur sprinted off towards it. There were queues of people filtering in, mostly oblivious to the wanderings of a dog.

The sign above the entry said *Please Do Not Feed the Animals,* but Arthur wouldn't care, he had eaten enough for now, all he wanted was water. Even the pavement felt hot under his pads, as he walked along the concrete ground. A pathway led along a winding stretch, allowing people to wander this way and that, in and out of hutches, hatches and hideaways for all kind of animals, birds and wildlife. The path led around a huge center, and back on itself again, with people moving slowly. Children walked alongside parents, each staring into dark places, standing back and watching life in all its ornate glory, dancing to its own tune, as long as it remained captive. Smiles abounded, skips and steps of avid wildlife lovers, as tamed and captive as they all were.

Arthur sniffed the air, scenting more animals and birds in one place than he had ever known. He had never truly known danger in his life, so anything truly wild and harmful to him would smell just the same as a tired old donkey, as likely to kick him as lick him.

"Mum, has one of the animals escaped?" a young girl asked. She had one hand held onto Mum, the other onto her ice cream, which through neglect and sun had melted all over her hand and arm. She squinted in the sun, trying to make out what kind of sheep it was that wandered around near them.

Mother looked up and around, to see Arthur licking the girl's hand.

"Oh, stop that," Mother said, tugging her daughter away. "No, honey, I don't think that belongs here."

If Arthur could understand what she had said, he might well have agreed, but wondered too just where he did belong. It seemed everyone laughed at him, never with him, and nobody wanted him.

Finally Arthur moved on, circling round the path, slightly interested in the small birds warbling and twittering on, fluttering around inanely, but none so interesting as to want to play. At the far end he could see something large and brown, like an overgrown version of himself. He jumped ahead, ignoring all the calls around him, avoiding the voices which appeared shocked and unsettled.

At the end of the path, in the corner stood a giant, not quite so like him, a pig in fact, its small curly tail betraying the fact that it was in fact huge. It moved this way and that, foraging for food amongst the dark wet mud, itself covered in an unfair proportion of it. Arthur stood, looking in, through the wire fencing, wondering what it was and what it intended to do. Suddenly the pig let out a slight but obvious grunt, at which Arthur's ears perked up, making the pig jump back a little. He couldn't decide whether the pig was offering to play or telling him to back off. It was a marvel, something he had never seen before, so large and round, and yet possibly playful.

Arthur yapped, ever so slightly, his own tail wagging in time with the porker. The pig ignored him, continuing to forage for anything it could find, which didn't include dogs, and would never include sharing.

"Hello boy," a kindly voice offered. At first Arthur wondered if it were aimed at the grubby pig, but as he looked around, he noticed a tall blonde-haired woman, wearing a plain white dress, mirrored by an equally plain white but huge hat across her head. She was looking at him, with such eyes he hadn't seen in an adult in too long. She was pleasant, and her demeanor suggested loving with it. Arthur turned away from the pig, his tail now wagging so much his whole body rocked in time with it.

"What's your name?" the woman asked, leaning over to inspect his collar. To her surprise he had none, unsure whether he had ever had one.

He had, but like so much of his former life, it had been lost along the way, leaving him unknown and at the mercy of the rivers of life.

Arthur licked the lady's hand with a dry sandpaper like tongue. He did it because it seemed the right thing to do, not because he had to, but also because it was the only way he could think of offering a reciprocal show of affection.

The woman moved her hand away from the dry tongue, instead patting him on the head. As much as he liked affection, he was never keen on head pats, much preferring a good scratch of his back. Arthur turned around, shoving his bottom towards her, as if to ask for a scratch.

"Oh no, I don't think so," the woman said, immediately pulling away. From the expression she gave it seemed she no longer liked him so much, at which point each stepped away from the other. Yet another person that for some odd reason didn't see just how adorable he was. At this rate, he would soon begin to doubt himself.

As he turned, he noticed for the first time several large birds in the center of the grounds. They stood near a huge white bowl, half filled with muddy water. All around were different types of birds, some small garden variety, others mere pigeons, some looking brightly colored. In amongst them all were rabbits, hopping to and fro, occasionally stopping to nibble on something between their paws, or simply lick themselves. What most caught Arthur's attention, however, was the water; muddy or not, it called to him.

Without another thought he ran quickly to the fence which surrounded the center. His eyes focused purely on the water, as it glittered in the bright sun. He loved how birds waddled up to it, before slipping into its coolness. How much he would love to do the same, all the while drinking form it. Arthur jumped up, front paws on the fence, looking across, wondering if he could jump right over and in. Nobody seemed to object, so he dropped down, stepped back and ran at the fence, jumping with all his might. All his might wasn't enough, as he feebly battered against the metal chain fence, bouncing off it and rolling around on the ground. By now people had begun to watch his actions, and as he jumped, dropped and rolled everyone laughed. He hadn't noticed he was being watched until then, and felt just a little embarrassed by his awkward failure, or as much as a dog can feel such things.

Still, he wouldn't be put off. Standing back up again he looked once again to the fence, ready to charge and leap like a gazelle, flying over the barrier to the promised land. Arthur went for it, running, leaping, front paws grabbing the top of the fence, ready to jump once again over, read for the lovely cool water, but as he topped the barrier, a wildly colored peacock sprang his way, its plumes firing out in a show of magnificent greens and blues, as if some kind of block, to say no chance. It squawked as he toppled this way and that on the fence, heaving, struggling not to fall again, or if he did, inside, towards the drink he so badly needed.

"Oy, you there, stop!" an angry voice shouted, disturbing Arthur's perfectly finely balancing act. He couldn't do anything else but look, to see a short, stocky man in green trousers and shirt, wearing a hat which screamed safari. He wore muddy wellies, and carried a dirty yellow bucket full of the smelliest food. He was coming Arthur's way, looking decidedly unhappy.

The choice wasn't great, either way he would fall off, look foolish, and end up the way he didn't want. He could go mud side, head towards the water, but there, between him and salvation was an angry green man, with a swaying bucket, who looked very much like he knew how to use it. On the other side was hard concrete, more laughter, and a terrible thirst which made his mind spin. When he had been home, his old home, the lady never saw him go without, always a bowl or a bucket here or there with clear, fine water. How he missed that now, how he missed her.

"Go on, out!" angry green man shouted, louder than ever. People no longer wanted to see the wild captured animals, all they wanted to see was this little dog, and the park ranger fending off the attacks of the wild beasts. All eyes were on Arthur, as he clung to the top of the waist height fence, as if he were on top of a cliff, ready to descend with perfect style into his inevitable future.

The crash was harsh and instant. Just as green man was about to either push him or grab him, Arthur did the decent thing and dropped. It wasn't far, but that didn't matter, all that mattered was the water was gone, and he was off again, parched, so thirsty he wondered if he had eaten a bowl of sand.

As Arthur dropped, rolled, stood up and sprang away, angry green man chased to the fence, shooing him away. Everyone broke out into applause, some wondering if it was a new show for Walton Gardens, the dog and the ranger, wild life in reality or something equally silly. Arthur didn't look back, but if he had he would have seen the over large ranger trying unsuccessfully to climb the fence to chase after him.

Once again Arthur was off running, seeking out an escape, hopefully to someone who wanted him.

*

By now the park was a mass of people, so many that few would notice a little dog running across the huge expanse of park grass. Those that would notice would reasonably think that it was someone's dog, brought to the park for the day, and escaped. Someone would come along soon to bring him to heel, get him on the leash, control him, but nobody would, not this dog.

Arthur ran right across the park, away from the enclosure, away from picnics and sunshine, towards high trees and massive bushes, any sense of shelter. Stone steps led up a hill, which he followed without a thought as to where he was heading. Right up he went, along a slender path, as masses of greenery encroached upon him.

His mind was all of a fuss, but as he climbed further up, the heat and the intensity of the day got to him. Lack of fluids finally brought him back down to Earth, as he panted heavily, struggling with a dry throat the likes of which he could never remember having.

The plants, bushes and trees surrounding him provided brief respite from the expansive heat, as flickering shades of light poked through, reminding him it was a good idea to wait where he was. It had been so much fun, so liberating and free to run from one group of people to the next, seeing their responses, happy or otherwise. Bits of food he had pinched here and there were equally welcome, but now all he could think about was to drink.

Slowly Arthur regained his composure, his lungs breathing easier, as the fine scent of roses filled his nose. In the far distance ahead, he could see rows of colors, beds of flowers all nearly aligned, with prim hedges surrounding them. It looked like a nice place to sleep, but he never could while being so thirsty.

Arthur's ears pricked as he heard a familiar sound, something which alerted him to memories of the past. He waited, holding his breath a moment, taking in every scent and sound, looking carefully back to where he had come from.

Bushes lined the edge of the path either side of him, but nothing prevented him from wandering into the undergrowth. Feeling curious to the noise nearby, he walked gently into the greenery, poking his head through, lifted large leaves away, feeling the soft, dense layer of dead leaves and debris under his paws as he carefully walked. He was eager, and playful, but for all his daftness, he was never quite so foolish as to charge ahead to a place he couldn't see.

The noise grew louder, becoming clearer as he walked, until finally he stepped out onto a large outgrown rock. The top of it felt wet to him, and immediately he began licking its surface, thankfully for any kind of moisture. As he stopped and looked, he could see the entire park as far as he could see, people all over, sitting on blankets, wandering around, children running and playing, everyone enjoying the sun, and no more dogs running around try to grab their food.

Arthur stood, feeling as if were in charge, commanding all that he could see, looking, wondering what to do next, until his attention focused on the sound of the noise. It was difficult to believe what he had missed, as water cascaded down a rockery, into a dark green pool, where the path went in opposite directions to create a circle with a welcoming pond in the center.

Arthur paced around, seeing how high it was, but desperate to get to the water. The cascading torrent was too steep to climb down, although his need was so great he simply had to try, stepping gently from one rock to the next, feeling how slippery it was. People were moving around the path near the bottom, all looking into the pond, watching as shapes under the surface moved to and fro. It all looked so inviting, so cool and pleasant, all he could think of was joining in on the fun.

"Mummy, what's that?" a voice called, as a little girl stood holding her mother's hand looked up, pointing. Mummy looked up to see Arthur stood atop the rock, surveying all he could see.

"It's the Lion King," Mummy replied, laughing as her daughter gave her a look of amazement. Her innocence was a wonder, how she could say something and she would instantly believe it. Long may such innocence last, she thought.

"No, darling, it's a dog, I guess he's a bit lost," she explained, as they both watched Arthur's show.

By then others had begun to notice, chatter increasing as people pointed to him. He was quite the sight, a panting dog, stood on a high rock, looking over at them all, pacing around as if he were stuck, but was in fact wanting to get into the water. For all his wily nature when it came to food and drink, he never did have the sense to simply go around, back down the path and lap at the water's edge.

"Hey," a voice shouted. Everyone turned to looked, as did Arthur, only to see green clothes man, the park ranger, looking at him in a way which made it clear he wasn't amused. "Get down off there," the ranger shouted, as if Arthur could clearly understand his instructions. Arthur had never been shouted at until his days on the streets, but lately it seemed to be the only thing people ever did.

The ranger was in no mood to wait, as he began walking briskly up the path, heading for the stray dog, a potential menace to all, and if not, then a good excuse to shout at someone for letting their dog off.

Arthur noticed his approach, realizing it was now or never. He had to find a way to the water, or get away. The green man strode with intent and purpose, his face a picture of annoyance, ready to set the world straight again. Dogs couldn't be allowed to invade the parks, and certainly not allowed to disturb the little fishes, not on his watch!

Arthur paced more and more urgently, lowering himself to the ground as if that would perhaps make the drop any less then the thirty feet that it was. The ranger finally got the edge of the path, then pushed bushes aside, stepping onto the soft ground. A few feet more and he would make a grab at Arthur, and no doubt take him away to much applause.

There he was, there was the little dog, standing there, as Arthur looked around to see the man heading for him, barely feet away.

Arthur stepped back, wondering if he should turn and scatter, try to elude him back onto the path and away in the opposite direction. Instinct took hold, an urgent need, just as the man grabbed at his neck, pinching hands onto his scruff. It was all over, the man would have him, Arthur was caught. Who knew where it would end.

As the man took a hold of Arthur, gaining a better grip, Arthur struggled, lightly at first, then more as the grip became tighter. The pressure around his neck became intense as the man struggled to get a grip of him, however he felt it necessary. Arthur would never bite anyone, or hurt them, so he couldn't help but be confused at why anyone would act towards him in any way other than pure kindness. He had a lot to learn.

Arthur pulled strongly, needing to be away, back to kind people, as the man lifted a hand quickly to grab him underneath. As he did so his boot flaked off the wet rocks, causing him to slip. Arthur took his moment, shaking and writhing, until he broke free. The ranger fell to the floor, before struggling to get up. Once again, he leapt at Arthur, only this time the small dog had become just a little bit wiser, turning quickly to the edge of the rock, breaking out into a short burst of speed before leaping off, out into the air.

The ranger turned, caught by surprise, grabbing at where he thought the dog had been, but no longer was, vanished into thin air. He stumbled, losing all control, slipping on the rocks, no longer in control of his destiny, much as Arthur was in no control of his life. The man went crashing down, sliding headfirst along the flowing water, down the rocks. The last thing he saw before he crashed into the murky waters below was Arthur, soaring through the air like some magical pooch that could fly.

Arthur leapt out, front paws stretched out as if he were jumping over barrels, tail pointed behind him, like a canine arrow heading as an Olympian swimmer, off to win gold at the Walton Gardens Olympics. The water buried his head as he created a tidal wave of a splash, sending a huge churn of water out across everyone, the whole crowd who had gathered to see the spectacle. It proved to be amazing and funny, but the price of admission was a good soaking, and all paid the price.

Arthur dropped into the water like a furry brick, creating a deluge that rippled around the pond. He dipped deeply under, swam for all his life, before coming back up, breaking through the surface like a brown submarine on a reconnaissance for supplies. He had what he needed, as his front paws lapped away, pulling him along, he lapped up with his tongue the cool, fresh water, as murky and as green as it was, it still tasted good.

It was worth it; he was instantly cooled down and at the same time felt so relieved as he drank of the waters. As he looked back, he saw green clothes ranger man at the side of the pond, dragging himself out, as water spilled from him like a leaking toilet.

Suddenly everyone broke out into applause, some shouting *more*. As children shouted, happiness and laughter abounded. It was a great day, Arthur was a star, albeit for a brief moment. He paddled on, until something in the water caught his eye. He stopped a moment to float, trying to see what it was. As he looked on, two round eyes came up from the depths, surprising him. Whatever it was it kept opening and closing its mouth, bobbing around, staring at him without blinking. Arthur was shocked, wondering what it might do to him. It was clearly time to get out, so he headed to the side.

His body was heavy, laden with water, making climbing out difficult. He lifted his front paws up, clawing at the edge, trying to gain traction. Finally, he gripped just enough, as a kind person helped, hands around his shoulders, pulling him. Slowly he lifted out, water dripping all over, as he looked around to see who had been so thankful. Now he was surrounded, not by kind people, but more green clothes people, as several park rangers had gathered. A loop of rope attached to a long stick connected over his head, and before he could shake himself free and run, he was snared.

"Got him," ranger man said proudly.

"Did you enjoy your swim?" another ranger asked him. He ignored the question, as if he were an army lieutenant having completed a major mission, and wouldn't have questions asked of him. Success, that was all that mattered.

"Mummy, where are they taking him?" the little girl asked, wondering what had happened to the Lion King.

"It's OK, darling, they will take him to the petting zoo and give him a home there," Mummy replied, smiling at her daughter to ease the concern.

"No, he won't," green clothes man said abruptly. "Dogs home for him," he said, feeling happy with himself.

Mummy gave him a stern look. "Pig," she said, taking her daughter's hand and walking away. Others followed suit, showing their disdain for his attitude. The crowd dissipated, having enjoyed the fun, but none too happy at being soaked.

Arthur struggled, but as much as he tried, he couldn't break free. The rope around his neck was too tight, and even if he did get away, there were large people on all sides, walking with him. Wherever he went next, he would be blocked, and the rope around him made it quite clear there was no escape this time.

For the first time since he had run away Arthur felt nervous, so nervous that he began to shake. As hot as the sun was, and refreshed as he should have felt, he knew the future from the point on was a mystery. He no longer had control of his own life, his own choices, and wherever he ended up, life would never be the same for him.

CHAPTER EVEVEN

Three weeks had passed. Three long, lonely weeks. Arthur lay, in his new home, in his new bed, shaking. It felt like he hadn't stopped shaking in the entire time.

A shadow cast across him, as the company in his new home paced around. This wasn't a kindly, loving person, there were no pats on the back, no sensitive voice, no treats or hugs. Stood over him was a large scruffy Alsatian, occasionally pacing around, sometimes stopping to look at him or sniff him. Once Arthur had tried to look at the dog, to make it clear he didn't like being sniffed in such a way, but the dog was big, and growled at him. Arthur had sunk back into his shell, trying not to think about how things were, only what was. Confusion was his bedfellow on the long nights since.

He lay on a muddy folded quilt, trying to ignore the foul smell coming from all around. Either side of his long home were riveted, silver metal fencing. As high as he could see, up to a white concrete ceiling. At the back lay another folded but dirty quilt, one which the bigger dog inhabited. Arthur never went near it. Up front was a tall metal gate, silver, with a heavy lock on it. The moment he had gone in he knew there would be no escape. It was as if he had been put away in a box, so they could forget about him.

As he lay down softly his mind wandered back again, thinking to that amazing day in the park, all the smiles, the fun and happiness. The walk with the rangers had been a long one, right across the place, as all eyes were on him, filled with pity but no interest in doing anything to help him. Parents and children could go about their lives, pretending he had simply got lost, and soon he would be reunited with his family and all would be good again. Sadly for him, that would never come true.

It had all happened so quickly. Tied to a fence away from others, then bundled into a truck, driven somewhere he had no idea where, and then out to this place. The first thing that hit him was the noise, dogs barking, dogs howling, dogs complaining endlessly. The second thing to hit him was the smell, such awful smells. The kind of thing that he was aware of when he went out walking, out in the fields, only he would scrape his back paws and cover it up, because that was how he was brought up. Not now, surrounded by all the worst of life for a dog.

Still, there was the food. Arthur perked up as a person walked to the front of the cage. It was the woman who came twice a day. Sometimes she had a kindly look about her, but sometimes she just seemed tired, and didn't even look at him. She would open up the gate, drop two bowls of food to the floor and leave them to it. First day in his home the other dog had eaten both bowls before he got a look in. Second day when Arthur tried to get a taste, big Alsatian growled his infamous growl, *leave me alone* it said. So, Arthur laid, and waited.

"Hey boys, got a visitor for you," the lady said to them both. Today she was in a good mood, which always helped, because if she was it meant they might get a run in a larger enclosure. Arthur still had hope, not much, but some.

The Alsatian as always sprang to the front, looking all around for food, or something good. Arthur lifted his head, but little more. Lack of food, lack of proper attention and love had made him weak. All he could see was a bare concrete yard out in front of his cell, and so stuck inside such a place, what need was there to do much?

The lady was dressed in jeans, and a baggy white sweatshirt. She wore wellies, well accustomed to the nature of the place. Her hair was a long, frizzy mess, her eyes, as blue as they were, still seemed tired. Dogs were her life, but sometimes that life affected her, on days when she couldn't do anything for them. Today, she hoped, would be different.

"Here they are," the lady explained, stepping aside and ushering in her guests.

Two adults and a child stepped in, but jumped back away again as a Rottweiler in the cell beside leapt at the fence, barking its heart out, demanding they back off. The family duly did. Perhaps another wasted opportunity.

As the family stepped away, a squat, short man stepped around them. He had all the natural appearance of a farmer. He wore wellington boots, with corduroy trousers held up by the ubiquitous piece of string. He had on a striped shirt, with missing buttons, and a wide-brimmed brown hat which had long seen better decades. He tried to bend over to gain a better look, but his huge stomach forbade such an action, and so instead simply stood, watching, without saying a word.

Moments passed, as the family stood awkwardly. The father held onto his daughter's shoulders, waiting patiently for the man to step aside so that they might try again. The man just continued to stare at the dogs, as if he had fallen asleep standing.

"Hi, would you like to look at some other dogs?" the lady asked, looking at the family, smiling feverishly.

"Er, yeah," the father agreed reluctantly. As they were about to turn away, the young girl tugged at his hand, looking at her knowingly.

"Actually, could we have a chance to say hello to this little man?" the father said, stopping still.

"Why yes, of course, we have an old tennis court, we can go take him to run around there and you can sit with him if you like. Which one?"

"That little brown one please, he looks a friendly chap."

While all the commotion was going on, Arthur remained laid, straight out, back legs pointing behind himself, front paws under his chin, looking and listening. The young girl looked like a kind, fun person. She wore such bright clothes, it seemed obvious to him she must be a bright, kind type of person. The older ones, the way they stood and smiled, they seemed to be the perfect people to be with. His heart beat faster, as he allowed himself to dream of a better life, back in a true home, filled with love, and full of the best things, such as nice treats and food.

"Hello, my name is Penny," the young girl offered, crouching down, looking directly at Arthur. The moment she looked at him, his tail began to wag eagerly. It was never deliberate, but he just couldn't help himself.

"You like him? What's your name again?" the lady asked.

"Penny," the young girl replied quietly, realizing she was the center of attention.

"Oh, that's a lovely name. My name is Sue," the lady suggested, smiling at her happily.

"Yeah, he'll do," the squat man said loudly.

"Excuse me," Sue asked, squinting as she looked at the man in farmer clothes properly. As much as she always tried to be positive to people, sometimes she couldn't help herself.

"That small dog there, he'll do, I'll take him."

"Well, these other people have already said," Sue insisted.

"Sorry, but I distinctly heard them say yes when you asked if they wanted to look at other dogs. I'm here, I can take him. He's mine."

The awkwardness went through the roof, as polite as Sue was, she felt awful, not wanting to upset anyone. Penny looked at her, and to her parents. She could just tell it wasn't going to be.

Nobody spoke. Everyone looked anywhere but at each other, except at the burly man, who was foraging in his pockets for screwed up cash.

"I've got the money, cash here, seventy pounds isn't it?" he asked, beginning to walk away. "I'll go pay at the desk; you bring him along."

As he walked away Sue looked down at Penny. "I'm so sorry, I should have said something."

"It's alright. He looks like he has a farm, so this dog will probably get plenty of space to run around, I think," Penny replied. As much as she tried to remain positive, she struggled to hide her feelings.

"Should we go, come back another day?" Penny's mother asked.

Both parents looked at one another, wondering what to do. Just as they were about to jump in and say something, Penny interrupted.

"Oh, he looks so sweet," she said, pointing to a small Yorkshire Terrier in another cage. While the adults had been feeling down, annoyed with themselves over not reacting quicker, Penny had already moved on, finding another lucky dog ready for a new home.

All three adults looked at each other, surprised but pleased, and moved on.

"If you go and look at another dog, I'll just take this one in for this gentleman and then be back in a moment," Sue suggested. Penny's parents looked at each other, relieved there would be no tears today. Probably.

Sue turned away, heading back to Arthur, reluctantly opening his cage. As much as she was pleased to see a stray dog getting a new home, she couldn't help but be disappointed at how things seemed to have turned out.

"Come on, boy," Sue said, kneeling down. The Alsatian charged at her, jumping two front paws onto her shoulders, licking her face madly.

"Phew, come on boy, that's enough," Sue struggled to say in between licks. For a dog so bad mannered, he was as equally loving. Being so large most had trouble dealing with it, but she was so used to dogs that it was fine, it made it all worthwhile.

Arthur by then had sat up, looking at them both, in his usual quiet manner. He simply looked, watching everything they did, wondering if he should join in, but not wanting to be too forward in case she raised her voice. In the weeks he had been there, she never had, but in the time since he left his old home, he had begun to realize how often people did shout, and how much he disliked it.

Amidst all the fuss and fury of Alsatian kisses, Sue looked away to see Arthur there. Her heart dropped, at the thought of where he might be going. As much as she wanted to say he wasn't available, she knew she couldn't afford to pass up a chance for the dog to have a home, and so whatever the outcome, this little dog was leaving them.

"OK, boy, in you go," Sue said, pushing the Alsatian back in. "Come on, come here," she continued to say, now looking at Arthur. As she looked at him, she clicked her fingers, beckoning him over. Arthur waited, unsure, not wanting to get in the way of the much bigger dog. The last thing he wanted was a fight. He didn't do fights, unless it was with a cuddly toy, and then he was a monster, able to take on anyone.

Finally, Arthur stood up, moving towards her slowly. Deftly, she placed one hand on Arthur, gently moving him out, all the while slowly pushing the larger dog back in. As she closed the cage door the Alsatian began to bark, making Arthur cringe. Even if it didn't last, he was glad to be away from the barking beast, and with any luck, away from the dog who kept pinching his food.

Sue placed a small, loose collar around his neck and attached a piece of cord to it. Arthur didn't disagree, hoping things would turn out better for him. It could hardly be worse.

As the two walked slowly up the hill back to the office, Arthur took a look back, hoping it would be his last there. All he could see were rows and rows of places similar to the one he had spent what seemed an eternity in. Dogs in most of them barked every time someone walked past, making the place seem so crazy. Until he had arrived, he had never seen so many dogs in one place.

"Here he is," the squat man said, standing at the office door holding it open.

"Would you like to have a sit and chat with him first, see how he is with you?" Sue asked hopefully.

"Nah, we're all good. I've paid, and we're ready to go."

Sue was surprised. It was rare someone took a dog without asking any questions or spending time with them. Warning signs were flashing in her mind, but as much as she was concerned, she couldn't escape the fact that so many dogs needed homes.

"Do you have your paperwork?" Sue asked.

"Er, yeah, they have it inside. You just need to sign it they said."

Sue nodded and headed through the door. As she did so the man smiled, such a fake smile she had never seen.

"This gentleman has just paid for this dog; do you have all the paperwork done?" Sue asked, looking at a younger man sat behind a desk. The man was stubbly, wearing what appeared to be a jacket denoting the dog's home. He seemed happy and relaxed about it all, quite the opposite of Sue.

Sue picked up the papers, leafing through the information given.

"Mister Barker," she asked, noting mentally that the man had given the name Barker, and wondered if perhaps his first name was dog.

"Yep, that's me," Barker replied, continuing to smile.

"Is the dog for family? He'll make a good family dog," Sue explained, looking the man in the eyes.

"No, no, just me, on a small farm holding. He'll have plenty of space to run." Sue allowed herself to believe what he said, that the dog should have a better life, no matter where he came from, if indeed the man was a real farmer.

"No name?" Barker asked.

"No, he was a stray. For some reason the previous owner didn't get him chipped. It's typical of older people, not to bother, and then if something happens to them, we often have no way of knowing what they were called."

The man looked around, barely interested in her information. He just wanted to get away.

"Do I get anything free?" the man asked, eyeing the food supplies and bags of items.

Sue had no desire to provide anything for him, but she looked at Arthur and could see how lost he looked, the sadness in his eyes, the fear, and figured anything to make his transition better.

"Not normally, but seeing as he's such a lovely dog, I'll give you this," she said, picking up a leather collar and lead from a rack nearby. There were rows of such items on sale, as well as food, all intended to make money to help feed the dogs. Such as Barker would never care for their needs, only for his own.

Sue removed the temporary collar from Arthur's neck replacing it with the new red one. She attached the lead to it and knelt down, looking Arthur in the eyes. Arthur mirrored her, sitting down, looking back at her, but unable to maintain eye contact. It was something he had never been able to do, looking directly at anyone, because there had never been the need. Finally, Sue pulled him in, pushed her arms around him and hugged tightly. Arthur closed his eyes, imagining for a moment he was back with her, that wonderful lady who had made his life so special. As much had he loved her, as much as he missed her, in those final few minutes with her, deep down he knew what was coming, and what had happened. When he ran, he did so not simply out of fear, but out of such heartbreaking sadness that he couldn't cope with. For that one short moment, hugging this lady, he was back there, feeling at peace again.

"Come on, I've got things to attend to," Barker said, interrupting them. As Sue stood up, she looked away a moment, allowing herself time to recompose herself.

"I'm so silly, so many come and go, and I can't help myself," she said smiling through the emotion.

"Thanks," Barker said, tugging on Arthur's collar, almost dragging him along.

It was a bad moment for Arthur, and for Sue, but sometimes life isn't perfect, and sometimes you just had to accept it, and try to adapt. Arthur was in for a new experience, one that would teach him more about surviving and people than he would ever want, but in time, it would set him up for his greatest adventure yet.

CHAPTER TWELVE

The road was bumpy. So bumpy it seemed as if any moment the truck would spill over sideways and fall completely over. Arthur remained sat in the back, on the smooth metal base, his lead attached to the back of a seat. The floor was muddy, clearly from carrying so many dirty things. As Barker drove his Jeep, the ground was unforgiving, but the truck even more so, with failed springs and broken suspension, every single rock, stone, bump and hole in the ground shocked them. Each time the truck veered down a hole Arthur slid across from one side of the truck to the other, then up a hill, he would slide right back down again, bumping into a corner each time.

"Will you sit still?" Barker shouted. He held tightly onto the steering wheel, stuck comfortably in his seat, belt on tight, used to the road and its highs and lows. Arthur wasn't, having no idea what to do. Every now and then he would scratch at the floor, trying to gain a better grip, but it was too smooth, too jerky, impossible to handle.

The truck hit a particularly large block, bumping and ticketing them so hard Arthur jumped up in the air, flying for a moment, only this time he didn't have the soft landing of a pond, but a hard metal floor to crash to. It was the worst, but there was worse to come.

Up ahead loomed a building, with a larger one to its side. As they slowly progressed up the dirt track, rain began to fall. At first it was just a smattering, but as they drove further, the rain opened up, becoming a deluge. Barker switched on his windscreen wipers, only to find one didn't work. He was thankful for small mercies, that the one working was on his side, otherwise he would have had to lean over.

Finally, the endless grinding stopped. Everything fell silent, except for the rain driving heavily against the screen. Arthur looked at Barker, as he turned to look back at him. However much he hoped, it clearly wasn't going to be good. Arthur trembled, wondering what was to come. He was in a dark place, any light in his life was slowly disappearing.

"I guess autumn is coming," Barker said loudly, leaning one arm over his chair, looking directly at his new pet. Arthur's ears perked up a moment, wondering if perhaps he was going to be nice after all.

"Just in time to be my perfect rat catcher," Barker said. The tone of his voice sounded anything but pleasant. Arthurs ears dropped again, along with his hopes.

"Right. Out," Barker shouted, straightening up, before opening his door and stepping out. The ground was a squelching mess, puddles everywhere as rain cascaded down. He walked around to the back of the truck, opened the side swinging door and leaned in. Arthur mistakenly wondered if he were about to get a hug, and wagged his tail incessantly. Instead Barker unfastened the lead and pulled on it. Without a thought at all to his new dog he yanked hard.

"Come on, out, I want to get inside," Barker shouted, pulling the lead so that Arthur was forced out. He dropped down uneasily, out of the dry safety of the truck, into the beckoning storm, in his life and from the weather.

Rain washed over Arthur's coat and he shook, trying to dry himself. It was a waste of time, as more rain cascaded down. He looked down at the ground, sniffing around himself. The air was full of unusual smells, all sorts of scents, many of which he had never experienced before. As difficult as it suggested it was going to be, he couldn't help but be intrigued by what was around the corner, literally.

Barker didn't say another word. He pulled his jacket tighter around himself, slamming the door. Yanking again on the lead he dragged Arthur across the yard, heading towards the huge building, a place which had once been a barn, but was now nothing more than a storage for junk. Leaning over, Barker grabbed hold of the end of a metal chain, fastening it to Arthur's new lead. Eventually it dropped to the floor with a clang.

"For seventy pounds you had better be a good rat catcher, boy, cos if you're not you won't be getting fed," Barker said, walking away.

Arthur watched him go, having no idea what he meant, but instinctively he had an idea of what was to come. He sat slowly, watching as Barker walked away, back into the house. The last thing he heard of him was a door slamming.

The skies were gray, and where before the wind had been warm and so full of light, everything around now seemed dark, as if he had entered a new place where such things no longer existed. He looked around as the rain fell ever harder, soaking his fur, dripping into his eyes. If he had tears to cry, they would have been washed away by the rain.

A chirping noise nearby interrupted his thoughts, piquing his interest. Arthur looked around, wondering what it might be. Silence again, other than the sound of rain hitting the large roof on the building near. Finally, it occurred to him to get up and walk a few feet, to get under cover. As he did, he was thankful to be away from the rain, but unfortunately for him, the smell was worse, like something he himself left behind when he did his business, but pretended it wasn't him.

Again the chirping sound presented itself to him. He looked, but the corner of the barn was dark, made all the more difficult to see due to old stacks of hay, oblong piles of them, tied up with string, clearly left for far too long. He stood up, noticing the chain sound, the weight of it dragging against his neck. It felt awful, but at least long enough that he might move.

The sound stopped, only for something to move nearby. Arthur watched, as pieces of straw ruffled around, nudging here and there as if it had come to life and was about to spring up into something surprising. The corner darkness slowly encroached on his position as shadows gathered. The wind and rain outside circled, as the storm gathered, all at once as if focusing on him. He was at the center of it all, the wind, the rain, the blistery blowing of the gale, the rush of water across his face and body. It was as if he had been placed inside a washing machine, with only his head stuck outside.

For all his travails, Arthur would never lose what little sense of playful humor he had been born with. He looked around, wondering where he could go to hide, but also at the many things he might discover in time. At least with all this water around he wouldn't be so thirsty again.

Far away, across the yard, through a wide metal gate, lay fields, empty fallow fields, full of dying wild flowers and overgrown weeds. Beyond them were tall swaying trees, and beyond further the skies opened out into a crack of blue expanse, where shards of sun threaded through, covering the distant landscape in glimpses of glory. It was a distant dream, one which beckoned to Arthur, the suggested peace, tranquility and love, somewhere in a place he had run from, and was yet to find his way back to. Whatever happened, Arthur was strong, and he would never give up.

The straw nearby ruffled again, as a tiny squeak made him jump a little. He sat, relaxing a moment as the roof finally provided a moment of respite, and clarity for his thoughts. It was smelly, but reasonably dry, and come what may, it seemed someone had taken him in. He would be fed, and given water, and perhaps in time get to go indoors and to know his new owner. No doubt about it, because deep down all dog owners are the kindest of people. Arthur thought so.

As the last drips of water eased from his coat, Arthur finally allowed himself the luxury of laying down. Slowly he edged down, front paws grabbing at the ground as he slunk lower. He licked his mouth a little, before taking time to clean himself. It was something he often did in his spare time, especially his paws. The thought of all that dirt in there, in every nook and cranny, in between his claws and pads, it didn't bear thinking about, so he would lick and clean, and in time feel canine again. Much better.

Squeak, the sound came again. Much louder. Arthur didn't jump this time, merely stopping mid lick. Time had allowed his eyes to adjust to the dying light, and before him was a small creature, its fur like his but much darker, sat hunched on its hind legs, front paws small and pink, scurrying around its pointed whiskered face.

Feeling curious, Arthur leaned in a little, doing what he always did best, sniffing. Arthur's nose matched that of the small furry creature, both peeking this way and that, only the small thing used its tiny front paws to wipe its face all over, as if eating an invisible peanut. The smell to him mirrored that of the place in which he laid, not the best, but not the worst he had known. The creature seemed simple, but harmless, and if need be, if there was a problem, he could simply bark at it, and it would no doubt scurry away.

Eek, the little creature went, then again, louder. Arthur sat up, wondering if it was time to show it who was boss. The furry thing stopped moving, watching as he towered over it, casting his own shadow of intent. The thing was a little too loud for his liking, as he stared it, it cried again and again. Time to show who was boss. Finally, Arthur stood right up, eyeing it. Just as he went to bark, something else caught his attention, something else moving nearby. At first he ignored it, focusing on the animal that might dare to challenge him. Then something else caught his eye, and another, until he had no choice but to look away. To his side, deeper into the open sided barn was another of the small creatures, also sat, looking at him, but beside that was another, stood out long on four paws, with its long pink tail flowing away from itself. Beside that was another, and another, and more, until as his eyes became accustomed to what he was seeing, he could see dozens of the things, all looking at him. As if a barnyard chorus had sprung up, and in unison, they all screeched, their wild *Eek*, as if a cry for battle.

Arthur's eyes widened as his heart pounded, as he suddenly realized he was outnumbered. Before any tiny thing could make a move for him, he sprang away, back into the whirlwind of rain and storm, to the gray clouds, back to the comfort and safety of being soaked and freezing.

Now he knew, the rats had a home, and he would be sharing it.

Arthur went to turn away, to look around for somewhere else to hide. As he did his head cracked into something unyielding.

"Hey bonehead, you're not supposed to run away, you're the one supposed to be terrorizing them. Go!" Barker said loudly. He was still in his wellington boots and baggy trousers, but he had changed his shirt into a checked one, and held an old tatty umbrella over his head. He looked at Arthur as someone would when they were preparing for an argument.

"Well go on then," Barker cried. Arthur lowered his head, upset at being shouted at. He wasn't used to it, and certainly not from people who were supposed to love him.

"Useless," Barker said, snarling at him. "You're as bad as that cat I got, wanting to lay around all day, and when I threw it in there it ended up hiding from the rats."

As Barker turned to walk away, his knee caught Arthur on the head, whether on purpose or accidentally. Arthur fell over, rolling a little in the puddles and mud, scrambling to get up. As he struggled to stand, and watched his new master walk away, the tiny light of hope in his heart that his new family might love him began to fade. With it went the hope that he might ever be loved again.

Barker walked back to the house as Arthur watched him. The house was stone, high roof, and looked cozy inside, as an open fire burned and a television played. Arthur watched as Barker went in, threw his umbrella one side and sat in a large padded chair. His life seemed reminiscent of the one he used to have, one which he had taken for granted, never knowing just how cruel life could be.

As the rain fell ever heavier, Arthur realized he couldn't stay outside, so began to look around. There was the barn, but that was taken, and there was the house, but he knew he wasn't welcome there. Off across the yard was the gate, and fields beyond, but nowhere to shelter. The pathway down the drive where they had entered looked inviting, but as he went to walk a little towards the opening, the tug and rattle of the chain attached to his new collar reminded him that he was going nowhere.

As the wind blew and the rain fell, it seemed as if there would be nowhere for him. The thought was terrible, that he might have to live outside. It was only then that he came to realize how important a home was, or at least, somewhere to hide, not just from the chill, but from people, neither of which were always so kind.

The bushes and trees surrounding the farm swayed, heaving to and fro. As they did, an opening near to the barn became obvious. It wasn't much, and mostly covered in greenery, mostly ivy, but Arthur spotted it, looking dark, and empty. As he thought about it and looked on, the wind grew ever stronger, until he had no choice. He began to walk, blown around, ears flapping about like mini kites in a hurricane. Rain splashed across his eyes as he blinked ferociously, trying to make out what it was. It was obvious, being so close to the barn that it might have someone or something living in there already, but he had to see.

Arthur nudged the dense ivy with his nose, before lifting a paw to scrape away. It was a smaller shed, quite empty, around ten feet square. Quite why it was empty he had no idea, but it seemed relatively dry, and far better than outside. Slowly he forced his way through the undergrowth, dragging his chain along like Marley escaping from his ghosts. The minute he was through everything changed, as the riotous noise outside quelled, and the rampaging rain ceased to be an issue. It was as if he had stepped onto another world, one full of elements designed to make him miserable, to another which seemed void of anything. As darkness of night surrounded him once more, all he could see were its four walls, its high sloped ceiling, and the dank, acrid smell that all of the farm's building seemed to hold.

It was far from perfect, a black stony floor to lie on, and the smell would eventually make him dizzy, but it was dry and warmer anyway. Arthur went right in, turned around a few times and lay down as best he could. From his new position he could just about make out the yard beyond as the storm waged its war. He shivered a little, wondering what the new day would bring, let alone every day after that. As ever, he hoped for the best.

CHAPTER THIRTEEN

Morning sun is always welcome, and no place is it more welcome than on a farm. It provides nourishment for new plants, allows new animals to be settled and at the very least, flowers flourish and life grows vibrantly all around.

As the sun climbed up over the horizon, so it swept away the last vestiges of the night before, drying as its crest touched upon damp roofs, wet walls, and slumbering dogs. Somehow Arthur had managed to fall into a deep, troubled sleep, whimpering away at all of his life's problems. Regardless of it all, he had closed his eyes and allowed himself the right to rest.

The drift of the ivy had covered him from the worst of the elements, but no matter how hard he had tried, he couldn't scrape the ground to become more comfortable. It was never going to be a perfect blanket to mold itself to his shape.

Another sudden noise outside woke him abruptly. The moment his bleary eyes opened to try and throw off the tiredness of the long night, he noticed the deep rays of sun touching the tip of his nose. It felt smartly welcoming, like a gentle hand reminding him of the beauty still there for him. Filling his senses was also the sickly-sweet smell of flowers, growing here and there, wafting in the fine breeze, giving off one last throw of dying summer as autumn took a firm hold. Leaves on trees beyond were clearly browning, not to mention those fine scented flowers looking not so much wild as decaying.

Arthur couldn't imagine how it might soon be for him, if still outside when the snows came. He had never experienced such a thing without shelter, and never wanted to.

A mild rumbling noise brought him further from his aching slumber, wondering what the day was bringing him, whatever he wanted. He lifted himself up, stretched as hard as he could, feeling every joint in his body. He became aware of muscles he hadn't known he had. As he stretched, he became aware of a fuss taking place outside, something that couldn't be ignored.

A stampeding sound came around and died again, as Arthur nudged his way past the overgrowth, out into the warming arms of the sun.

The sunlight was so bright it made him squint, but as he stood, apart from the joy of warmth, he wondered about something to eat. His stomach reminded him of the hunger that ate away at him. Whatever happened next, he would need to find something, or hopefully, his new master, if not friend, might come round soon and feed him.

Arthur walked forward a little, stretching again. As he did, movement across the yard near the gate caught his eye, something large moving quickly. He walked on some more, reminded of the chain as it dragged a heavy weight against his neck. It clanked mildly as it dragged across the stone yard, like an albatross around his neck, some kind of punishment for being naughty in a way he had yet to understand. Perhaps diving into the pond hadn't been such a great idea after all.

Again the sound came, like thunder hitting the ground. Arthur was curious, so made his way towards it, closer to the gate. As he stood looking through the huge, wide metal gate, he could see a white horse running around, galloping playfully by itself. It reminded him of all the times the lady had taken him to such fields, allowing him to run free, how much fun days like that could be.

As the horse ran so freely, all he wanted to do was leap over the gate and join in. Arthur stood back a little, ready to launch himself, but as he did the chain rattled, dropping links to the floor, reminding him he was attached to something, not emotionally, but physically.

It was a wonderful thing to see, such a large, strong white horse, running around with such joy. As Arthur watched on, he spotted something else appear, a bundle of grayish-brown fluffy scampering across the field. It had long flappy ears, and bounced across as it went. The bundle of fur ran up to the horse, looking up, before running quickly away again, back to a mound of wild grass and disappearing.

The field seemed to be a source of life, as butterflies flittered around and insects filled the skies darting all over. Dying wild flowers let loose embers of petals and seeds, their last natural attempt to spread and pollinate. The place was like a quilt of life, where one could jump straight into it and wrap oneself in all the beauty of creation. In Arthur's mind he was running around in it already, making new friends, rolling around on his back on the soft grass and chasing butterflies as the one who loved him the most looked on and laughed, providing a chorus of happiness that was missing from his life.

"Boy, if you want to get fed, you'd better get working, rat catching," a voice said harshly.

Arthur looked around quickly, to see Barker walking past. He held a bucket in his hand, filled with fresh fish. The aroma was strong, though they were uncooked, he might still be tempted to have a nibble, as his grumbling stomach reminded him it was still there.

"Well," Barker said, as Arthur stared at him. "Go get some rats, cos you won't eat 'til you do," he said aggressively. At first Arthur had thought the man might have been playing with him, but he could understand enough from his tone, and certain words such as *eat* that if he wanted food, he would have to find his own.

Barker walked to the truck he had brought Arthur in, opened the door and dropped the bucket to the passenger side, before jumping in on the other side. He revved up its engine, as a plume of foul black smoke filled the yard, and headed off down the track. Arthur watched as he left, confused by his own self, happy that the man who shouted was gone, but afraid that he might not return. Arthur whimpered, sounding like a frightened child crying. He was struck even by the sound of his own voice, at the expression of his own emotion, feeling things he never knew he could; fear, hunger, and loneliness. It would shape him for the rest of his life.

Whatever happened next, he knew deep down something had to change, something big had to happen. Without another thought Arthur lunged ahead, back towards the track, following the man. He ran, building up speed, free at last, until the chain became taut, dragging him back so harshly it sent him flying. He fell, sprawling to the ground, but this time was different, he felt different. He wasn't going to slink away and give in, he was going to fight back, not with anger, but with strength, to find his way, there in the yard, and in life.

He looked around again, seeing so few options. For the moment he would go into his place, and hide, and think. The end of the chain remained fastened tightly to the corner of the barn, a tall thick pole so high up he wondered if he could ever see the top. The chain itself seemed so thick, he could never bite through it. He pawed at it a moment, confirming that it was so solid, nothing could break it. Even with his fine teeth he could never get through it.

Arthur drifted to his small hole in the yard, back through the overgrowth, and laid, looking out. His mind raced, as he wondered what next, for food, for freedom. As much as he thought, at the back of his mind, at least he had shelter.

The silence of the farm was interrupted as the truck came screeching around the corner, stopping suddenly, with Barker jumping out, minus his bucket. He looked over at Arthur, his head stuck out, each staring at the other.

"Oh right, so you found a place to hide have you?" Barker said loudly, laughing at his new pet. "We'll see about that."

Barker went through his front door, slamming it hard, leaving the sound of his boots stamping away quickly. Arthur waited, looking around, wondering if he would pop out suddenly, but he never would.

As much as it was a difficult situation to be in, at least he had somewhere to hide.

A rumbling sound erupted, as the small building he hid in began to shake. Arthur wanted to stand up, to move away, but his fear was such that he was stuck, not knowing what to do.

Suddenly Barker appeared through his front door. "So matey, you like your new home?" he shouted, smiling unpleasantly.

Now there was no choice, either hide away amidst the huge noise, or run out to the waiting arms of the man he feared more than anything.

Whatever Arthur chose, he couldn't win, as the rumbling sound proved itself to him, as a deluge of water gushed out from an opening high up.

He was blanketed in it, like an entire swimming pool being dropped on him all at once.

Arthur ran out, dragging his chain, as water sloshed all around him.

"Welcome to the cleaning pen, little doggy," Barker shouted, forcing himself to laugh.

Arthur was afraid, but he was determined, feeling a new sense of strength that he had only finally discovered. He wouldn't give in any more, nobody would be cruel to him again. He ran, hard, away from the flow of water as it cascaded and died away, away from the man to the mud track they had entered on. The chain once again instantly became tight, only this time he remained standing, holding his ground.

"No, stupid dog, no escape for you," Barker said, no longer laughing.

Arthur walked quickly to him, as Barker looked on, bewildered, wondering if the dog would be foolish enough to go for a hug. He would get some contact but it wouldn't be a hug. Instead of getting close, Arthur turned again, once again breaking out into a run, quicker now, bursting ahead. This time it was different, as the chain tightened so hard, the pole shook, the chain vibrating, the barn roof rattling with it as birds sat atop flew away in shock.

"What, hey, no," Barker shouted, chasing after Arthur. The small dog suddenly didn't seem so small, as he evaded capture, running around the man, dragging his chain. Barker fell head first, dropping down as the chain swept his feet away. Arthur changed direction instantly, running once again for the track. Again, the chain tightened, with more force than ever, only this time Arthur continued to pull, rising up, using his hind legs to pull and fight to be free.

"Stop!" Barker pleaded, now sounding the one afraid. Too late, as the chain tightened and flicked rigid again and again, the tall pole vibrated, and rocked, and shook, until rusty, neglected fastenings snapped. The pole fell, heading towards Barker as the roof collapsed, sides inwards, the entire barn crashing down.

"Nooooo," Barker shouted loudly, holding his arm above himself as if to protect himself. The pole smacked the ground hard next to him, making him flinch, before bouncing again and again off the hard floor.

As Barker watched his barn crash to the floor and the pole bounce around next to him, from the corner of his eye all he could see was a not so little dog fight for all it was worth to be free.

"No, you're not going anywhere. You'll pay for that," Barker snarled. It was never in Arthur's nature to respond in kind, and never would be, but when it came to his right to have a good and decent life, he would run and fight and be free, whatever the cost.

The chain became limp, sliding along the yard as Arthur saw his chance, moving away quickly with it in tow.

"No, get back here," Barker screamed. He spun over, grabbing at it for all he was worth. He tugged on it hard, dragging Arthur back, pulling him closer. "Come on," he shouted, determined there would be a price to pay.

Arthur knew it was now or never, refusing to give up, he struggled, throwing himself all over, flailing around like a wild thing. There was no going back, no matter what the cost.

"Get, here," Barker demanded, struggling to control the dog, pulling as hard as he could as the two fought for what each wanted.

The chain grew shorter, as Barker pulled it in, until Arthur for all his struggles was a few feet away.

"Here," was all Barker said, gripping the chain so tightly his hands grew white. Any second and he would make sure there were no more struggles.

Barker reached out one hand, ready to grab the dog, his dog, to do what he wanted. Arthur looked on, writhing and fighting with all his might, as snap, the collar broke, sending both of them flying in opposite directions. Barker looked up at the sky a moment, before the thought took hold to get up, quickly, grab him, stop him.

As he twisted and jumped up, ready to lunge out, all he could see was Arthur's tail as he ran for all his life into the woods and away down the track.

Barker looked at his truck, ready to scramble in and give chase, but before he could do anything, the last remaining side of his barn collapsed, falling sideways, as he looked on in horror at its total collapse, onto his cottage, crashing into the roof, destroying them both in the process.

Crashing sounds welcomed themselves to Arthur as he ran, his tongue lolling and flicking out as he ran so fast that he felt like the horse, running in the fields, enjoying life so much, as the sun returned to warm his heart. He was free, free again, and no matter what, whatever it took, he would never be anyone's pet again.

CHAPTER FOURTEEN

The brisk run of freedom that coursed through his veins helped him on. He had no idea where he was or where he was going, all that mattered was that he wasn't chained up any longer, and to boot didn't even have a collar on. Arthur trotted, like a show pony, muzzle in the air, as if he were all full of colors and about to win first prize.

Now, he was no longer the same pooch that ran out of the lady's house and off into a haze of ignorance. This was an all new dog, brand spanking new, all newfound awareness and sensibilities. Nothing could stop him now. If he could slip on some spandex and a headband, he would do backflips and dance to his own tune. From humble beginnings, he had developed into his own canine, unstoppable, and fully understanding of what he wanted.

What would be perfect for a dog like Arthur? Well of course, first and foremost it would be a loving home. It didn't matter who was in the home, man or woman, boy or girl, whichever age, as long as they were nice people. He could return the love of a good family, as much as they chose to give him. He was like a dog with the mind of an old hound, but the heart of a puppy, all hidden away dreams of love and affection, and yet aware that the world wasn't all sweetness and roses. Some things about him would never change, such as his ability to love without question. What had changed was his immediate acceptance. Now, anyone who wanted to see that flash of caring and wily instincts to hug, they would have to earn it, and it would take time.

Some things no longer mattered, such as where to, or what was in the way of wherever that was. Such things as cars. Arthur strode along, his back legs almost outpacing his front so that his bottom, tail high up in the air almost sidled alongside him, legs arguing with each other over who was going first. If he had gone on much longer, he may well have ended up walking sideways.

Before any such thing could happen, the blaring sound of a car horn interrupted his splendor, as he wandered inanely out into the road, wondering whether to go back again, his nose caught the sense of something wondrous, something that called to him, its name, food! The horn blared again, then tooted several short times in succession for good measure. Eventually Arthur cottoned on there was a noise and looked around, to see an angry man, window down, arm leaning out waving at him. It was too good a day to worry about anything, so Arthur just sniffed the air once or twice, his way of thanking the man for his kind gestures.

The road was long and winding, much like the one he had begun on, when he had run in the fields and become lost. He stopped a moment, dead center in the road as the car sped off and silence prevailed. Trees lined either side of the road, with steep, well-tended grass verges all along. A fine flowery scent couldn't hide the smell filling his nostrils, perhaps cooking chicken, or something equally meaty.

Arthur's mind lit up at the thought, only this time it wasn't at the behest of his grumbling, moaning stomach, it was down to his surroundings. His eyes connected with a memory, an image of a memory, a reminder of everything before. He could go on, ahead, quickly, and there he would find it, home at long, long last.

Arthur's paws hurt from all the walking, but none of that would matter if he could get home again. He sprinted, ignoring the panting he was doing from being out of breath, ignoring his hungry stomach, all that mattered was he was nearly back again. Trees flew past as he ran, cars rounded him as he ran down the middle, but all the while he was oblivious to it.

As he ran, he could see something at the end of the road, as the road moved round in a bend in either direction. The further he went, the more it looked familiar. He was close now, he could tell. Either way, one way home, the other, well he would go back and find home again anyway.

Eventually the roundabout came into view, a small circular thing, a round thing surrounded by mounds of grass and a gray pole on top with a light that wasn't on. It all seemed so right. Arthur stopped, looking one way, then the next. To his left led another road, this one with much steeper banks, up to some trees, possibly to the fields he knew and home. The other, to something that called him, a faint awe-inspiring smell, something tasty and wonderful.

Without a care in the world Arthur just sat, ignoring cars moving around him, or horns blaring, anyone shouting. All that mattered was he took his own good time over it and had a good think. Once again he sniffed the air, taking in all the scents, allowing himself to think back. Images flashed through his mind again, of long days sleeping, a full belly and cuddly toys to play with. Then, there she was, that lovely image of the wonderful loving woman who raised him. She was so kind, so attentive, and most importantly of all, she was always there. Always. Until now. Arthur felt himself sink a little, his body no longer so filled with pride and joy, as deep down, instinctively he knew the truth. There would be no going back, no love to return to. Life had changed, and there was no going back. There was no going left up that road.

Arthur took one last long looked down the road, looked up as the trees swayed heavily in the wind, as browning leaves scurried haphazardly around, as autumn fell upon the land, and in his life. The memories of her would remind him who he was, and what he believed in as a dog, and how to love, but for now, his destiny lay in another direction, and he knew it.

Arthur looked away, before running onto the pavement, and off in search of food!

CHAPTER FIFTEEN

"Yeah, well I said to her, it's no good leaving things out, I mean they might go rotten, in the sun."

"What sun?"

"Well you never know."

"Or someone could pinch them."

"Nobody does that, thankfully, not round here."

As the two chatted, they were so engrossed in conversation, they missed Arthur being stood near their market stall, as heated, cooked chicken sat on display, covered in the tastiest sauce. Or so Arthur thought, as he sat licking at the side of one particularly large piece.

"Bit quiet today," Elsie said, arms folded, standing. It was still quite warm, even though autumn was in full flow. She wore a full-length apron, the same one she had worn for thirty five years, even though it had worn so threadbare it looked like tissue paper. It had been good enough for her mother, and would be good enough for her. Stains and all. Her hair was fastened up so tightly her eyebrows lifted, but she was clean, the customer could see that, so it was fine.

"Aye, could do with a bit more trade. I'd really like to get a couple more sales to finish off today," Dan said. He appeared much like the woman beside him, only his apron was leather, but beyond that he too kept his hair fastened up, only behind a nice white netted hat, for cleanliness. His eyes were only on Elsie though, having stood on the market stall next to her for eighteen years, and in all that time never having the courage to ask her out. His was an unrequited love, sadly for them both.

"Would just like to shift one or more items, a piece of lamb, or a chicken maybe," Elsie replied, looking at Dan, wondering if he might finally ask her out.

As the two stood, silently, each waiting for the other to speak, both their attention wandered, as if their minds were linked, in unison, until both settled to look at the same thing. There, sat politely, and ever so quietly, was a little brown dog, with a small black muzzle, looking so cute and loving. Each would have gladly given him a morsel, a little treat, if it weren't for the fact that Arthur was sat there, looking at them with such large loving eyes, struggling to hold onto the whole chicken he had picked up, and was deftly holding in his mouth, sauce dripping down his chest.

And so it began.

It took a moment or two, with both Dan and Elsie looking at the little dog, wondering what was so odd about the picture. Elsie couldn't quite grasp such a small dog holding onto such a large chicken, where Dan couldn't understand where any dog could get such a nice tender chicken as that. All the while Arthur sat looking, wondering what his next move might be. He had come to accept it wouldn't all fit in his mouth, eaten at once, so had wondered if perhaps he should slink down and begin nibbling. The moment before he had gone to do just that, he noticed both of them looking at him, and so there they were, the three of them, looking at each other, all wondering.

"Elsie," Dan said.

"Yes."

"Isn't that one of yours?" Dan asked.

Elsie furrowed her brow, as fireworks erupted in her mind. Shock ignited between both of them, finally as it sank in what had happened. That small spark was enough, as Arthur gripped tightly on the chicken, turned quickly and sprinted away.

"Hey, come back with that chicken!" Dan shouted, trying to run after him. It was hardly the best way to be when chasing a dog with a chicken in its mouth, as for work Dan always wore thick, heavy-soled boots, so as he ran, he clopped more than bounced, thudded more than chased, and got nowhere in good time.

Elsie gave up on the chase before it had begun, not best pleased she had lost a chicken, but her mind had moved on, as she watched Dan try to be the man, waddling away in his overall and work boots. She broke out laughing, chuckling away to herself over it, and later, Dan would do the same, as they shared a private joke about that cheeky dog.

Arthur, he ran out of the market, having not been noticed before, now he was. As he galloped along, pieces of freshly cooked chicken dropped off, alongside a trail of sauce. It was too good, and he couldn't resist stopping for a moment to lick at it, supping some of the sauce into his mouth, nibbling at the chicken. When he had been at home, he had never been allowed to have a whole chicken with the bones, even though the smell was amazing, but now he had it all, and didn't know what to do with it. He grabbed at a particularly juicy piece, pulling it off with his teeth before swallowing it. It was the best food he had tasted in so long; he knew it would be a firm favorite. If he ever saw such a thing again, he would most certainly enjoy it all.

"Oy," a voice called. Arthur looked up to see a man stood at the door to the market. It was time to run, as Arthur grabbed the chicken and ran, galloping off down the street with chicken flaking off all over. Everyone who saw it that day commented on how odd it was seeing a dog running along with that in its mouth. Some even wondered if it was a joke, but Arthur knew it wasn't, it was the beginning of the new dog, one who knew how to look out for himself.

The man stopped at the doorway, regretting shouting as he did. As he waited and watched the dog run, Elsie slipped beside him, looking out together.

"You never caught him then?" she asked, looked at Dan with a smile.

"No, but I wish I hadn't tried to now?"

"Oh, why, you didn't do yourself a mischief did you?" Elsie asked.

"No, no not at all," Dan replied, looking at her, his expression not mirroring her enjoyment of the moment. Elsie simply waited, looking again as Arthur ran away as if without a care in the world.

"It wasn't until I actually looked properly, that I saw how thin he was. You could see his ribs through his sides, poor thing," Dan said quietly. It was one of the things she loved about him, how he would always be there, trying to be the man, but had such a gentle side to him.

"Poor thing. I guess he'll be having a good meal today anyway," Elsie replied. Dan laughed with her, looking at her a moment, as he always did, wondering if today was the day he would ask her. It wasn't.

"How about you and me go out for the night, to celebrate our generosity towards that little dog?" Elsie asked, finally putting him out of his misery. It had been the perfect moment.

Dan looked at her, not the least shocked. "OK," he stumbled to say, trying not to blush.

As for Arthur, well he was running so fast he dropped most of the chicken, and so missed out on all the dangerous chicken bones. Still, he had a taste for what was good, and wanted more.

It was good to run, as the heat had abated and rain began to pour. It was warm with it, so he didn't mind. As he ran, he splashed through puddles, feeling like a little puppy again, only not falling over so much. As he ran to a corner, a built-up roundabout with traffic moving in all directions, he stopped. The road had sunk, allowing a large pool of water to fill. It was perfect, as if it had been made just for him to be there at the right time. He leaned over the curb, sniffing at it, feeling thirsty, so decided it was fine, go for it. He tried to lap at the inviting water, leaning down, but the curb was simply too high. Bit by bit he edged further over, leaning down as best he could, but still too much. Finally, he stood up, edging forward, leaning out a paw. If he had to, he would stand in the puddle and drink, quickly, before anyone blared a horn at him.

The nagging thirst was too much, so in he went, simply setting to walk into the water. Arthur had no idea what cones were, and couldn't see signs, so when he walked into the puddle, he had no idea it was a burst water main, and a hole dug to fix it, so fell right in up to his neck, as the water engulfed him. One minute he was stood on the road, paw out, ready to walk into a puddle, next thing he was submerged, diving for treasure.

Arthur flapped around, panicked to the surface and scratched his way from the firm edge until he managed to climb out. As was his way, he stood looking around, hoping no one had seen him make a fool of himself. He was so naive and foolish in so many ways, but when it came to his appearance, he was always self-aware, could never be deliberately seen to be the fool. He stood there, dripping, before shaking it all off. He was soaking wet, and had still not had a drink. He gave it up, walking off again, pretending it had never happened.

The road wound around, shops on one side, with traffic flowing on all four roads in each direction. The huge shop near to him was a gym, something he didn't like the look of, full of sweaty people looking as if they were running to escape but unlike him didn't know how. No matter, he was sure they would get wherever they were heading eventually.

One road further down had less traffic, so Arthur decided to wait for his chance. He ran along, looking all the while, waiting for his moment to run across. It wasn't so much a matter of whether the timing was right, because the only timing that ever mattered to him was when to eat, when to wee and when to sleep, and now none of those times were there. What mattered was when the time was right for him to run and pretend nothing was coming, like most dogs do.

Then and there, for no other apparent reason than that he felt like it, Arthur turned a quick right, looking out at the road. A long single decker bus appeared, and stopped, pulling up slowly, like the parting of the Red Sea, waiting for the chosen one to cross. As if in sync, a driver of a car coming the opposite way also slowed, as each waited for him to cross. Arthur had grown wily, and smart when he needed to be, but had the presence of mind to cross when given the chance. He dared to look either side of himself, noticing the bus driver, looking directly at him, smiling broadly. Arthur wondered if he might be so kind as to offer him a home, or at the very least a chicken, but then as he had learned, people could be unpredictable, so perhaps he should just move on.

Once he was across, the bus and cars all moved quietly on again, each enjoying the unexpectedly interesting moment that life had brought them.

Arthur's nose once again filled with the scent of food, as his belly called for him to act. It seemed the perfect place to be, an entire row of small shops, all selling different foods. The first he came to appeared like the large place he had found himself in, rows and rows of hard things which he knew he could never chew into. That was one worth avoiding. Next up seemed empty, but the following one had a door open, with its window stacked ceiling high with white boxes covered in red squiggly splashes.

He stopped, because the smell was so intense, it was difficult to ignore. It was a combination of meaty smells, many of which he was familiar with, and other smells, cheese and sauces, some of which were new to him. It was a heady mix, one which seemed to whisper to him, *come inside*.

As he waited and looked, he could see a huge, shiny, silver metal counter, too high to see over, but also allowing him to be shielded. He sniffed, his nose bouncing up and down as he gulped in the fine pleasures of the aroma. Ahead inside the shop was a small square worktop acting as a barrier to entry, but beneath was open, as if it were designed just for him to walk right on through. So he did.

It seemed as if the place were empty, as nobody appeared round back. He looked up, to see cupboards and worktops high up. On top of the edge appeared something fluffy and white, something he had never seen before. He sniffed at it, as was his way, to find an unusual smell, of pizza base which he had never known before. As with anything for him lately, it was worth a try, so Arthur jumped, quietly lifting up until his front paws just about reached the edge of the counter. Then, his eyes lit up like illuminations, as he found the counter full of pastry, vegetables, meats, chicken pieces, all sorts. It was like his birthday all at once, a banquet of possibilities, all prepared and laid out for him to rejoice.

Then Arthur heard a sound, whistling, coming from the front of the shop.

"Wow, it's raining, and too hot, all at the same time, crazy weather," the man said, trying to whistle and mumble to himself simultaneously. He looked around, completely oblivious to his surroundings. It had been a long two years, having gone to live in another country, hoping to find a better life, only to find himself working in exactly the kind of place he had left. Still, it paid the bills, and was better than working in a factory.

Antonio was a cool looking character, never fazed by life, and always relaxed. He wore a striped t-shirt, covered in sauce stains, even though on top of it he wore a long white apron. His jeans were years old, and his trainers needed replacing, but his love of music meant all of his money went on that. His hair was a wild, thick mop of curly black, all tied up haphazardly into a bun, and covered with a floppy white chef's cap. As always, and every day, he walked around in his own little world, looking at food all day, while listening to music. Today was no different, as he wore a small headset, sounds beating out into his ears, filling his imagination with ideas. It was all his own work, and sometimes he would take inspiration that others he would just enjoy. Today was all about inspiration, as he sought to create a new track for what he hoped would be his breakout mix tape.

Arthur was divided, unsure whether to grab and run, or to wait and see how the reaction would be. Before he could choose, Antonio wandered past, clicking his fingers and bouncing along. The two passed as if leaves drifting in a flow or rain down a street. It was as if there were a magic, invisible barrier between them, where one could see the other but the other couldn't even see the room, let alone a stray dog.

Any moment now, Arthur expected a shouting match to begin, as the man spotted and chased him, or he would bend over and give him some love, which he knew full well would never happen, but he could dream, doggy dreams, such innocence.

"Get my back..." Antonio sang. Arthur thought he was shouting at him, not that of a happy man singing. He had no time to move, and little inclination, still wondering if he might get some food before the fun began. The man plonked down a bunch of onions he had been carrying, lifted a knife from a block on the counter, and began peeling and chopping, continuing to sing.

As the man worked away, feverishly, as if he had no time but too much to do, he dropped something to the floor. He bent over, fumbled around with his hand, all the while not looking at what he was doing, too busy singing to himself, chopping away at anything and everything.

It looked red, and smelt decent, so Arthur quietly walked over and licked at it, before nibbling it, then taking it into his mouth and chewing it. It was meat after all, uncooked, but still, beggars can't be choosers. Anything would do.

Once again, he stepped back, still not sure how the man would react. Antonio gave up feeling around for the food, leaving it alone. Besides, it would be dirty anyway. He resumed his work, flinging pizza bases down, smearing sauce on and covering them with toppings.

"Take my baby back..." Antonio sang particularly loudly, occasionally playing air guitar with his hands, dropping bits of tomatoes and meat chunks as his arms swung around. Each time a piece flew off Arthur ran quickly over and grabbed it, gobbling it up.

Arthur had no idea why the man was so kind, but he certainly was, singing to him all the while dropping him some food. Perhaps he had noticed him after all, and seen how hungry he was, so was doing what all kind people did, feed them.

Antonio stopped what he was doing, looked up ahead of himself and began clicking his fingers, dancing to the tune in his head. Arthur sat, wondering what it was about, but more concerned at the lack of ongoing food. Suddenly the man spun around. As he did Arthur stood again, wagging his tail, expecting a fuss, and perhaps some love. He liked this man, he was odd, but fun with it.

As if there was nothing to see the pizza man continued to sing, one hand clicking fingers, the other dropping bits of meat and cheese all round. Each time a pizza was full he lifted it carefully and dropped it onto a large metal try in an oven beside himself. It was a daily ritual, one that wasn't always fun, but it paid the bills anyway.

Again another piece of music lifted his spirits, and he just had to dance. He pranced, one foot in front then back, the same opposite foot, lost in his own world, as Arthur watched the fun. Slowly the pizza man began to turn, enjoying the music, looking around, loving the moment. He looked at Arthur, and as he did Arthur began to wag his tail fiercely, wondering when the hugs would begin.

"Great music eh, puppy?" Antonio asked, smiling broadly. If only dogs could love music as much as he did. He continued to dance in his own little world, turning back to his food creations. It was all too much for Arthur, he couldn't take the teasing over food anymore, so barked, once, then again louder.

Antonio continued to dance, until suddenly it occurred to him, dog! He spun around abruptly, looking directly at the small brown dog, wagging its tail so happily at him, mouth open, tongue hanging out, looking at it so expectantly.

"Dog," Antonio shouted, suddenly feeling an overwhelming sense of panic. Arthur barked again, as if to say yep, me, dog.

"Nooooo," Antonio shouted, suddenly no longer so enjoying his music. He began waving frantically, trying to shoo him out.

"Hey, Ant, have you finished up..." a loud voice called. Antonio's eyes went wide as sheer panic set in. It was his boss, Juno, back from a very long, very liquid lunch, same as every day. Arthur barked again at the sound, then more for food, almost bouncing from joy at what could be his new home.

Juno lifted the table top cover, walking through to the cooking area. Immediately he clapped eyes on Arthur, as the happy dog turned to say welcome to him too, to our new home, all were welcome.

"Antonio," Juno asked, as his employee looked at him, wide eyed and full of fear.

"Yes Juno," Antonio replied, quiet as a mouse.

"Why do you have a dog in my pizza restaurant?" Juno asked, his tone measured and succinct.

"Well, er, well it's not a..." Antonio stuttered.

"Not, not what? Not a dog?" Juno demanded, his voice rising.

"No, er it's not a restaurant, it's a parlor," Antonio replied, wishing he could think of something else to say.

"Really? You think it's funny?" Juno demanded. He moved towards the large counter and picked up a long, black handled knife. Antonio backed away, trying not to trip over Arthur, who was still expecting great things.

"Now, Juno," Antonio began as Juno began grabbing utensils from the top. He picked up a bowl of grated cheese the threw it directly at Antonio. Antonio ducked, moving nimbly out of the way. He was many things, but one of them was certainly a fast learner. Today's lesson was he was going to lose his job, and the second lesson was to get out, quickly.

"No, don't leave Antonio, I still have some things to throw at you," Juno shouted, grabbing anything he could lay his hands on. By the time he had finished his sentence, Antonio was outside the shop.

Juno looked at Arthur, as he returned the favor. "Hey little doggie, would you like some food?" he asked.

Arthur looked at him, before barking, fully understanding he had used the magic word, food.

"I'll give you food," Juno shouted, bellowing at the top of his very powerful lungs. A tiny trickle of doubt crept into Arthur's mind, as he saw the look in his eyes, mirroring that of the farmer before. Finally, he had learned that not everyone was so nice, so decided to use his new found wisdom, and move on. Quickly he jumped forward, grabbed a slither of meat off the floor, gobbled it down while looking at Juno, as if to say, *I'll have this first before leaving,* after which turning to run.

Juno grabbed at anything he could find, picking it up and chasing after the escaping dog. He trundled out of the shop to see Arthur on the pavement, having stopped to see one last time if he had been wrong to run.

"You want food, little doggie, have this," Juno shouted, throwing a large fourteen inch pizza as hard as he could. The entire thing spun, saucer style, landing squarely on Arthur's head, covering him like a wide brimmed hat at Ascot Races.

It all went dark as he was covered in pizza, but it smelled lovely, and he just wanted a nibble. As he leaned his head down to the ground the pizza rolled off, giving him a chance to see and lick at it. Any hopes of a fine feast of a meal were interrupted as Juno came charging at him. That was it, the final straw, he had to go, so turned and ran, feeling most let down, not at the lack of food, but the loss of what he had hoped would be his new home.

Without another thought, or another care in the world, Arthur ran, straight away, across the road, ignoring screeching cars and blaring horns again, over the small roundabout, back onto the road the other side, ignoring the bus driver who had stopped, knowing it was the same dog he had seen earlier, and carried on running. Off he ran up the street as Juno shouted, cars beeped, and everyone watched.

Arthur was off again, running wherever, he had no idea, but it had to end, soon.

The road passed right along where he ran, the other side grass and more shops. In the distance he could hear shouts and screams, horns blaring, but the further he went, the quieter it became. Up ahead was another road, which he crossed, ignoring anything in his way, luckily lines of traffic all stuck and waiting. Across he went, over the grass, no longer bothering to look where he was going. Finally, he headed for houses, into a long dark alley, overgrown with bushes and weeds. He was becoming out of breath and wondering where it would all end. No matter how much he smiled, no matter how much he wagged his tail, or how much affection he showed, nobody seemed to return the favor.

Arthur slowed, beginning to wonder if anyone would ever love him again.

He trotted on, feeling tired, but no matter what, he would never stop trying, because it was in his nature to go on, to keep trying, to keep looking.

As he passed halfway down the alley, he noticed an opening in the brick wall, leading to somewhere even darker. He stopped a moment, lifting his leg, while giving himself time to recover his breath, and have a sniff.

The darkness inside the hole gave nothing away, no suggestion as to whether it was safe, or dangerous. His senses told him nothing. All his sniffing told him was that it was mildly damp. With nothing to lose and darkness threatening to come in, he headed slowly into the gap, treading softly, feeling every part of the bumpy ground underneath. As he walked through, it opened out into a larger building, full of broken windows and rubbish strewn all over. As he walked to the center of the large room, he noticed the floor was hard, but most of all it was warm, and dry enough. He sat a moment, looking around, listening, occasionally sniffing. It seemed there was no one around, and nothing to be afraid of. It didn't matter how long he stayed, but for now, he could find peace.

Arthur turned in a circle, tucked his tail beneath himself, and laid down, ready to sleep and forget it all.

CHAPTER SIXTEEN

Memories were hard to come by of an early age. Images in Arthur's mind showed little glimpses of how it had been, two people, smiling at him, full of kindness and caring, but the images were fleeting, slipping away into his dreams.

Further on, ahead in time, things were clearer, running around in circles as she smiled at him, the loving, care-free smile. It meant everything, because instinctively he knew it was heartfelt, joyous and innocent, like he was. Not quite so innocent any more.

He could smell something. It wasn't really there, now it only existed in his dreams, and his hidden, secret hopes. The smell was of almonds, and fine scents of flowers, that certain perfume of hers too, when she hugged him, he would close his eyes, and feel like a newborn again each and every time, wrapped up in cotton wool, sharing a common sense of love.

There were two of them, but he wasn't quite the same, not so many hugs, but still, he loved him so much too. He would throw something, a ball or a stick, and shout to him, not at him, and together they would share that moment of fun, where one would laugh, and he would bark, and run, grabbing it, returning it. Then he would run back, get a pat on the back, knowing he had done well, and together their bond was inseparable. Nothing could divide any of them, nothing could change things between them, except time.

Petals and pollen from flowers drifted through Arthur's mind as hazy sun warmed his body and love without question filled his heart. He was a dog born of affection, and nurtured on boundless moments of being together.

Whatever time did to them, to that special lady, or him, whatever anyone else said or did, nobody could ever take that away from him. He had regrets, as he lay on the concrete floor, all alone, but in his dreams Arthur would never be alone.

CHAPTER SEVENTEEN

It was dark, so dark even with allowing his eyes to adjust nothing could be seen. It was cold too, colder than he could ever remember it. Autumn was in full swing, creeping over the land like a blanket covering color, leaving only gray dampness to see and feel.

Arthur raised his head up. He had slept, uneasily, and felt the strongest tint of chill air. For all he was inside, the smashed windows let everything in, and the floor was hard, too much to bear. He knew though, that he had no choice.

Something caught his attention, a flickering from the corner of his eye. As he looked around and up, he could see a mass of tiny lights just beyond, rising up to the dark sky, like a fine stilted tree, all in a line, lights moving up, so bright and inviting, so welcoming. Arthur laid his head down again, allowing his eyes to focus on the sight, as he could see dozens of windows. Some had curtains across them, others were open, but all seemed so inviting and most importantly warm.

As he stared, he noticed someone walk to the one of the windows, looking out, before quickly dragging long curtains across. The light still spilled out, but no longer so bright and welcoming. He laid, wondering what it might be like to be inside there. It would be warm, quiet, safe, but would they welcome him? Probably not.

Still, it was a magical sight for a dog, laid alone in such a harsh, empty place. He laid looking at it a while longer, before tiredness dragged him back to a difficult sleep.

Boom.

Arthur woke up so quickly his vision spun. Whatever had made the noise had done it so loudly that the ground shook.

Boom.

Again it shook, only now he looked around, trying urgently to see what was causing havoc. He had put up with so much, but now he had no answers, nowhere to go. He felt as small as he really was, looking up and around, wondering what might happen any moment.

Boom, the sound came again, only now a small round ball hit into the large wall before him. Glass shattered to the ground as bricks and rubble fell down. The noise stopped as a white helmet with a man underneath peered through.

Arthur stood stiffly up, looking at the man, as he noticed him in return.

"Woah, hold on, there's a dog in here," the man shouted, turning and waving his hands. The noise stopped as an engine died outside.

"Hey boy, come on," the man said, leaning over slightly, walking towards him.

Fear had taken hold of Arthur, and trust was finally gone. Before the man could lean down to hug him, Arthur leapt up and away, through the gap that had been created and away.

"Hey, hold on," the man shouted, but Arthur was having none of it. He was off again, back on the road, in search of a home that wasn't being wrecked, where nobody shouted, and where they could share the kind of love he was capable of.

Off he went, out back across the grass, ignoring the workers and their machines, off over the road, ignoring the blaring cars, the frightened old lady who had been shopping, and off down the street.

"Hey," a voice called, as car horns screamed at him, as an old lady complained, Arthur panicked. Off he went, running, desperately trying to find safety, for love, happiness and a home.

Arthur ran, and ran, and ran, and disappeared from them all, straight under a little boy's bed. Of course, we all know how that ended, don't we!

Arthur, such a lucky, lucky little dog.

Did you enjoy this book?

If you did, please consider leaving a review on the Amazon website. Good reviews encourage writers to write as well as helping to promote our creative works to others. Whether it is a few words or a few sentences, if you could spend a few moments of your time with this it would be much appreciated.

Thank you.

Made in the USA
Monee, IL
09 June 2020

32374589R00062